Sign up for our newsletter to hear
about new and upcoming releases.

www.ylva-publishing.com

OTHER BOOKS BY KD WILLIAMSON

Cops and Docs Series:
Blurred Lines
Crossing Lines
Between the Lines

Pink

KD WILLIAMSON

DEDICATION

To my wife Michelle, I'd have nothing if I didn't have you.

ACKNOWLEDGEMENT

Thanks: to Maria for pissing me off and firing me up when I needed to be, so I could find my way through yet another set of characters; to Jove Belle for never mincing words; to my mother, who should probably never read any of my books—just keep them on the shelf.

CHAPTER 1

THE SUN REFLECTED OFF THE window, obscuring the view of the shop inside. Still, Shawn was hyperaware of the products on display. She shuffled her feet and coughed but didn't move toward the door. In the window, she caught the reflection of Veda's easy smile, as if she frequented sex-toy stores all the time. Well, Veda *did* used to work there, but did she have to look so damned comfortable?

Stepping back, Shawn took a good, long look at the building. Unlike all the other businesses on Canal Street, this one was a little more hidden away. It was tucked between two other structures and farther back from the sidewalk. There was a shabby neon sign on top. One S was dim, leaving "tumpy's" illuminated. "Why is the building pink?"

Veda snorted. "Because it's New Orleans and nothing normal happens here. You've only been here two weeks. Just wait. You'll see. It took me a month to figure it out."

Shawn rolled her eyes and sighed. She took a minute to try to shake the tension out of her arms, but it didn't help. If somebody bumped into her right now, she'd shatter from all the built-up pressure in her muscles. "I don't know if I can do this. I mean, I'm not shy, but I don't think I can scan and bag porn with a smile on my face."

Veda threw a hand up. Her expression was pinched and aggravated, but her blue eyes were soft and worried. "That's, like, the sixth time you've said something like that in the past hour. Gotta be some kind of record."

"Compared to what?"

Veda shrugged and wiped at the sweat that was dotting her chest and forehead. The lacy green tank top didn't look like it was helping her at all against this weather. The heat was oppressive, and the sun was a wicked master. It kept on shining like it didn't give a damn. Then, there was the humidity. It left Shawn sticky and wet. And not in a good way.

"I should've done the ponytail thing too. I'm gonna be able to wring my dreadlocks out by the time we get back to Metairie."

Veda arched a brow. "With all that hair, it wouldn't have helped."

Shawn lifted her hair off the back of her neck to improve airflow. To add to the misery, there was the ever-persistent joy of a farmer's tan. Shawn's arms, legs, and face were already two shades darker than her usual golden brown. Unfortunately, black people got sunburned too. It was a good thing she remembered to put on sunscreen or she'd be in even more trouble with this weather.

A small group of people walked around them and into the shop. Behind them, the chatter from the crowded sidewalk mingled with the clank of streetcars and honking car horns. Shawn loved the sounds of downtown New Orleans. The tangy smell of garbage and vomit, not so much. While New Orleans had its charm, Metairie was more her speed. Their townhouse and the surrounding area was cleaner, quieter, and, she hoped, safer.

"I know this isn't where you expected to be in life, but keep telling yourself that it's temporary. It's easier to find a job when you already have one, even if it's shitty. On the bright side, it's an easy job. You don't have to go all Vanna White with the merchandise. Just take their money. Most of them get tokens to go in the back anyway."

"Eww, that's…" Shawn refused to get caught up in the particulars. "It *is* just temporary, isn't it?"

Veda nodded. "It is, but don't put it on your resume."

The little speech should have emboldened Shawn, but it didn't. All she could think about was how she'd arrived at this moment. Like a well-deflated balloon, she sank in on herself. She was in a new city, with a new job, and a new life, which was a lot to wrap her head around. Despite having Veda, it was going to take a while to get settled, and a couple weeks wasn't nearly long enough. "She's gonna hire me right? There's no reason not to, especially with your recommendation."

Veda's eyebrows shot up on her forehead. "You used to be confident… hell, even cocky, and now you're like mashed potatoes."

That stung, but it was the truth. "Ugh, thank you so much, I feel like I can take on the world now."

"You know what I mean. I'm not saying that to be an ass. You need some—"

"Truth. Yeah, I know." Shawn needed to get away from this subject, otherwise she was going to be a mess for the interview. Nowadays, she was way more emotional than she used to be. "Are the floors sticky? I bet they are."

"They are, but you'll be mopping them to keep the stick factor down. Don't look too closely at anything you find there."

Shawn stared at her. "You know you just said that out loud, right?"

"Uh-huh. Look, I'm cooking out here and, while I appreciate porn and crotchless panties, I'm tired of standing and staring. We still have a few minutes, but let's go in. There's AC."

Shawn nodded. "Okay, you sure they don't have anything at Taco Bell?"

"Like I told you, they only pay seven twenty-five an hour so…no. Not for you. Now, if you could be a shift manager like me, that'd be a different story. You'd actually get a salary, but you don't have the experience." Veda pulled the door open. It creaked loudly.

"Fine, but let it be known, I don't like you right now."

Veda glanced over her shoulder. Her gaze went from Shawn's head to her feet and back again. She didn't look impressed. "Like I care."

The door closed behind them. Shawn pressed her lips together and stared at her surroundings. She was no prude by any means, but damn. Damn. There was a huge selection of vibrators and dildos in various sizes and colors. Some shelves were lined with magazines and DVDs. A blow-up doll in a sex swing hung from the ceiling, swaying softly. Shawn expected the place to smell like Lysol, but instead there was a faint tinge of apples and cinnamon.

It was…interesting.

Toward the back, the hallway was separated from the main area by a subway-like turnstile. It was dark, but there were flashes of light every few seconds.

Veda elbowed her. "You're staring and your mouth is open. Stop it. You're gonna make me look bad."

"I'm sorry. It's just—"

"Fucking. That's all. Ways to fuck and make it feel better. You do remember what fucking is, right?"

Shawn glared.

Veda smiled. "Still not liking me, I see." She didn't wait for Shawn to comment. She jerked her head toward the woman behind the well-protected cash register. "That's Phyllis."

The woman was hidden behind wood and glass. There were pieces strategically cut out of the window so Phyllis could talk, hear and exchange merchandise for money.

"Thank you. Enjoy and remember, no refunds." Phyllis's voice was high pitched and matched her appearance perfectly. She was tiny and innocent looking. Behind her glasses, her eyes widened when she saw them. Phyllis waved and gave them a toothy smile.

"*That's* Phyllis?"

"Uh-huh. You're staring again." Veda waved back.

"She looks like a librarian."

"This is a library…kinda, but you have to pay for everything."

Shawn met Veda's gaze. "That glass is always half-full for you isn't it?"

"Most of the time, yes. Here she comes. Don't embarrass me."

This time Shawn was aware of it when her mouth fell open. "You do see where we are, right?"

"You're being ungrateful, and you're way too far up on your high horse." Veda's smile dimmed considerably. She exhaled noisily. "Look." Her tone went all gentle. "We've discussed this until we were both blue in the face. This situation is shitty and kinda uncomfortable. It's not where you wanna be, but it's your best option right now until something better comes along. So, take it or leave it, but no more complaining now that we're here, please."

She was right. "Yeah, sorry." Shawn's flash of shame quickly turned to anger aimed toward the Midwest, specifically at her ex, Courtney, who was responsible for her shitty predicament.

Veda wrapped her hand around Shawn's arm. "Wherever you went, you need to come back."

Shawn shook her head, pulling herself from a haze of feelings.

Three loud clicks sounded in quick succession before Phyllis opened the door to her little wooden fort. That seemed like a lot of locks, but Shawn didn't dare point that out.

Veda dragged Shawn toward Phyllis.

"Hey, my baby!" Phyllis's voice dripped with enthusiasm.

Pasting on a smile was almost easy for Shawn. Veda did the same, only hers was probably real. She held out her hand for Phyllis, but she knocked it away and pulled Veda into a hug instead. Veda released Shawn's arm to return the embrace. "Heyyy!"

Veda was tall, thick and hippy. Phyllis had to turn her head to the side otherwise she would've ended up with a face full of boob. Looking away, Shawn pressed her lips together to keep from laughing.

Phyllis stepped back, but kept her arm around Veda as she held out her hand. "You must be Shawnna Green?"

"I am, but you can call me Shawn." She returned Phyllis's handshake.

"V called me at the right time. I haven't even advertised the job yet. You got lucky."

She was lucky, and appreciative. It was time to pull the stick out of her ass and swallow down the little pride she had left. Just because she had two college degrees didn't mean she was too good for this. Hell, for anything. "I know. Thank you so much. Is there an application or something I need to fill out before we start the interview?"

"There is. We can go up in the office and get situated. I've only got a few questions, and since this one here can vouch for you…" Phyllis leaned into Veda. "Tomorrow I'll start you on a trial basis at minimum wage. If you can hack it for two weeks, I'll bump you up to ten."

"That's too sweet, Phyllis." Veda's eyes widened.

"Oh hush, least I can do. You helped me through a tough time."

"All I did was listen."

"Well that's exactly what I needed, Ms. King, exactly," Phyllis said.

Shawn watched the exchange, but she wasn't surprised. Veda was incredible. She knew when to push, when to pull, and when to back the fuck away.

"Let's get on with it, then. I got customers. I'll wait on them while you do the application. Follow me."

Shawn nodded and did as she was told. "No problem. Thanks again for this."

Veda stayed behind. When Shawn glanced over her shoulder at her, Veda grinned, and she tried to concentrate on that instead of the huge display of porn mags behind her.

Shawn scooted toward the window. The metal was cool against her side. The bus had been late, but it showed up right before she melted. Veda sat down beside her.

"Well, that was easy."

Shawn hummed in agreement. "I have a question, though."

Veda grumbled. "Fine."

"Is Phyllis the genius behind Stumpy's? Or is she a figurehead like Ronald McDonald or something?" Shawn tried like hell to hide her grin, but she wasn't all that successful.

Veda blinked. "You're not allowed to speak again until we get home."

Shawn kept on smiling and looked out the window. This was shaping up to be one of the better days she'd had since moving from Indianapolis. She needed something to go smoothly after the whole Courtney situation. It wasn't easy starting a whole new life. As the bus ate up the miles, the scenery whizzed past Shawn until it was a moving blob of colors.

"Stop."

Caught by surprise, Shawn jumped and turned quickly. "What?"

"You're thinking about her."

She wasn't going to lie about it. "Yeah."

Veda grabbed her hand and squeezed. "I know I've said this before, but I need you to understand that I'm not kidding. If I ever get ahold of that ex of yours, I'm gonna put my foot so far up her ass she'll know my shoe size just by swallowing. I fucking hate what she's done to you. I knew she didn't have any common sense. The tiny forehead was a dead giveaway."

Part of Shawn wanted to laugh, but the rest of her tried to pull away. Veda wouldn't let her. "It's not all on her. It takes two—"

"Do you need to talk to my foot too? I have on sandals right now so you'll be able to taste the leather."

Shawn clutched at Veda's hand in return. "No, I…" She stopped herself from responding further because it wasn't going to be pretty. Shawn didn't want to seem any weaker than she already was.

"Something good just happened. Enjoy it, or try to. You should also look forward to all the tips you'll probably get. Flash that smile and maybe a little cleavage too. Hell, some of the customers might even try to pay you to smack them around a little."

It was very hard to stay somber around Veda. She had a way of sniffing it out like a bloodhound. So, for the moment, she let the morose thoughts go. Shawn stared at Veda.

"What? What did I say?"

"Do you wanna talk to *my* foot?" Shawn asked.

Veda laughed. "I'm serious. With those big brown doe eyes and those tits, you might make a killing." Veda glanced down at Shawn's breasts, making Shawn look as well. Her nipples hardened and pitched a little tent in the front of her T-shirt, as if they knew they were being discussed.

"Look at that. It's like fingers pointing at you."

Shawn crossed her arms over her chest. "Shut up!"

"Might wanna tape those things. Could put an eye out." Veda's pink lips curved into a wide smile.

Shawn laughed and pushed Veda away.

"Better?" Veda's gaze was full of amusement and understanding.

"Better."

Shawn got comfortable in her bed, laptop open and ready to go. Even though she'd already checked her email from her phone, she did it again on the computer. There was nothing to see. No responses to her resume, despite years of experience working with kids with mental health issues. Still, she had a job and should have felt at least a small sense of accomplishment, but she didn't.

She opened a browser and checked her ever-dwindling bank account. Shawn had enough to pay rent and her part of the bills for at least two months, if she squinted. Her mood fell further into the toilet, but she didn't want to be there. Set on clawing her way out of gloom, Shawn fired up Netflix and scanned her queue quickly, trying to avoid the movies and TV shows Courtney had added. Shawn couldn't bring herself to delete them. Not yet. She settled on the BBC series *Black Mirror*. The lives of the people depicted were a damn sight worse than hers. The British really knew how to entertain. A horror movie or a good thriller was usually her thing, but she needed a break from that every once in a while.

"In for the night?"

Shawn looked up to see Veda standing in the doorway. She'd changed clothes and was now in a different frilly top and shorts. "I guess."

"It's barely four o'clock. You know that, right? Didn't you promise me a few hours ago for the umpteenth time that you were gonna try to be a little more lively?"

"V." Shawn sighed irritably. She knew what was coming.

"Don't V me. I know that tone. You only use it when I'm getting on your nerves." Veda stepped into the bedroom. "You've been hiding in this room since you got here."

"I'm not hiding."

Veda raised a brow and pursed her lips. "What would you like to call it then?"

Shawn didn't feel like doing this. She didn't have the energy. "Resting. I'm fucking tired. It feels like I've been wrung out." She shook her head. "I'm probably not explaining it right."

Veda sat on the bed. "You are. You're not the only woman who got cheated on and dumped. I'm sure there's some statistic that shows it happens every nine minutes or something."

"I know what I went through is nothing new, but I'm me. This has never happened to me before, that I know of, and I'm dealing with it my way." Shawn closed the computer and pushed it off her lap.

"I get that, but you picked up and moved to Louisiana for a reason. You need support and to be around somebody who actually understands you."

"I know that too." Shawn looked down at her hands.

"Good. Then listen to what I'm saying. Get your ass up. You've wallowed long enough. I know you still care about her, but you guys were over way before she started cheating on you. This isn't you. You're strong, confident, charming, and funny. You have to get that back, and it's not gonna happen by staring at your computer." Veda's words had fire behind them, but her gaze was sincere.

"That's the me you knew back at Indiana U. I've chang—"

"Bullshit. Even after I left, we were on the phone every other day. Don't try to sell me that line of crap. I *know* you."

Shawn swallowed. Veda was right about everything. Shawn didn't even recognize herself. Instead of responding, she looked at her.

Pink

"Oh, honey." Veda patted her on the leg.

"The thing that hurt the worst was that I wasn't enough for her and then there were all the lies. It's good that I don't love her anymore." Shawn clenched her hands. "I feel… I don't know, but I still think about her a lot. It's been over a month since I've seen or talked to her."

Veda squeezed her knee. "That's progress, then. I'm off tonight. We won't do the tourist thing because it's muggy as hell and you live here now. But, let's get out and do *something*. We can celebrate your job, as pissy as it is. I'll google the lesbian hot spots and—"

"I don't think I'm ready for something like that."

"Okay, let's see where the men hang out, then. You probably won't have to worry about anybody hitting on you every two minutes."

Shawn snorted. Maybe she could have pulled that off back in college, but now? Veda was obviously smoking something.

"What? I'm serious. Have you seen you?"

"I know what I look like, thank you."

"Well, I know I've joked about it a million times, but this is a million and one. I'm not kidding. If I were a lesbian and saw those dreads, eyes, that smile, and experienced that brain of yours, I'd be all over you, trying to make you forget whatshername."

Shawn was flattered. Veda talked about her like she was the black, female version of Casanova. She smiled. "Thanks."

"So, are we going out? I'm sure I can find somewhere that's not over the top."

Shawn took a deep breath and nodded. She wasn't ready to jump in the water, but getting her toes wet was probably what she needed. Maybe it would help her feel less out of sorts.

"Good." Veda pulled the ponytail holder out of her hair and shook it loose. Being blonde suited her. She'd let her hair grow since the last time Shawn saw her, but it worked. When she wore her hair down, it framed her face in a way that brought attention to her high, chiseled cheekbones. Up in a ponytail, it was like seeing the freshman version of Veda all over again. "I get to play dress up. I haven't been out in a while. It feels like all I do is work. Gay men complimenting me would make me feel like Miss America. I could use some of that right now."

So could Shawn.

CHAPTER 2

GOOD FRIENDS. THE NAME SUITED the bar. It was small, cozy, and had a piano. Shawn wouldn't have been comfortable with strobe lights, throbbing music, and the press of gyrating bodies. There were plenty of men of various ages and only a handful of women. Shawn sipped the last of her vodka cranberry and wished it had been a bit fruitier. She glanced up in time to see Veda heading back to their table with new drinks. She wasn't alone. Two men trailed behind her.

Veda sat down with a big smile and flushed face. "Okay, this one"—she put her hand on the shoulder of the man closest to her and he leaned into the touch like they'd known each other forever—"is Mr. Leather 2013, and this"—the other man scooted closer to Shawn—"is Mr. Leather 2015."

Shawn smiled, but it felt awkward, like that part of her face was stiff. Mr. Leather. What the hell did they get for winning *that* contest? Shawn decided she didn't really want to know. She was a bit rusty and wasn't sure what to say. Courtney had been a homebody, and Shawn had become one as well in the five years they were together. It had been a while since she'd reached out to make new friends. "Uh…"

"There's no way we broke her already. We haven't said anything." Mr. Leather 2013 smirked.

"She's fine. Let's just say we're on the path of rediscovery." Veda pushed a fresh vodka cranberry toward Shawn.

She took a huge swallow. "Sorry. I really do know how to speak."

"Good to know." Mr. Leather 2015 chugged on his beer before setting it down. "I'm Jaime and that's Brad."

"Shhh, leave her be. I think the aloof butch thing works for her." Brad waved Jaime's words away.

"Plus, those cheekbones and lips." Jaime grinned.

Shawn's face heated and her gaze went from one man to the other. Then, she glanced at Veda. Her drink was pressed against her lips, but Shawn saw the smile in her eyes.

"They'd eat you up at GrrlSpot." Jaime continued to grin at her.

It felt good as hell to hear all that, especially from strangers. Still. "I'm not ready for that."

"Break up?" Jaime asked.

Shawn nodded. "Yeah, almost two months ago."

"Baby steps, then," he encouraged.

"I'll make out with you if that'll help." Brad smiled saucily.

Veda laughed. It was loud, boisterous, and Shawn couldn't help but be pulled in by it.

When she was able to get her amusement down to a chuckle, Shawn held up her drink to Brad. "Thanks for the offer, but I don't kiss—"

"Men," he interrupted. "Shame. I don't discriminate, especially with the hot ones."

Warmth gushed through Shawn, and she did her best to hang on to it. "Next round's on Veda."

Shawn and the Mr. Leathers laughed. Veda glared.

Jaime finished his beer. "No, drink up, everybody. I'll get the next one."

Twenty minutes later, Shawn was laughing so hard she couldn't breathe. "No way."

"I'm not kidding. I'm a nurse. I wouldn't lie about this kind of shit. It broke off inside her. I can understand a cucumber, but a frozen smoked sausage? That was a disaster waiting to happen."

"Obviously, she needed to go grocery shopping," Veda snarked, which sent them into laughing fits all over again.

Brad stood. "Okay, hold on. No more stories till I get back. Anybody else want a refill?"

Everyone raised their hand.

"Well, shit. I need help then."

"Let me pee, and I'll help," Jaime offered.

When they were alone, Shawn felt Veda's gaze. She glanced at her.

"You're having fun."

"I am," Shawn agreed.

"Told you so."

"You did." Their outing had been way better than any BBC show.

"Fuck Courtney."

Shawn actually smiled. The pain didn't cut as deep. Maybe it was the drinks. Maybe it was the company. Maybe it was that she'd let herself enjoy life, even if only for a few hours. She held up her glass. There was only a sip left, but she tilted it toward Veda. "Fuck Courtney."

Brad smiled and set a new drink in front of Shawn. She muttered her thanks.

"Okay, you see that woman at the bar? The light-skinned one with the short curly hair and the blue shirt?"

They all turned to look.

"Don't look!" he hissed.

"What, why?" Shawn asked.

"She asked me about you."

"Oh." Three sets of eyes zeroed in on Shawn.

"She's one of the hot ones too," Brad said.

They were all still staring at her. Shawn took a sip of her drink. "Thanks for letting me know." It was getting uncomfortably warm, and she was pretty sure the drinks weren't completely responsible. Shawn's stomach churned, and her heart raced. She was flattered but full of anxiety too.

"Shawn, this is exactly what you—"

"No. I haven't done the casual thing since college, and it wasn't all it was cracked up to be. You know me better than that, V."

"No one's saying you have to fuck her. Go talk to her. It's nice feeling wanted every once in a while," Brad chimed in.

Jaime was suspiciously quiet. He turned his head from side to side like he was watching a tennis match.

Shawn glanced toward the bar. The woman in the blue shirt was staring right at her. She was definitely one of the hot ones—Halle Berry hot, complete with smoky eyes, high, angular cheekbones, and full red lips. She smiled, and Shawn swallowed, hard. "I wouldn't even know what to say. It's been years—"

"Well, you've already proven you know how to speak. I think you'll figure it out," Veda interrupted. "Courtney moved on, and you have to start somewhere."

"Kiss for luck?" Brad smiled crookedly. "Last chance."

Shawn chuckled and realized that this was the most carefree she'd felt in months. She stood. She could so do this. What was the worst that could happen? Rejection? Being laughed at? Shawn's alcohol and group-induced bravado went down a notch.

Someone grabbed her hand, and Shawn glanced down.

"Stop it. Don't think, just do it," Veda said.

Veda's words put the brakes on her thoughts. Shawn nodded. She picked up her glass, intending to take a sip, but three vodka drinks were enough. The buzz she was feeling was nice, and she didn't want to screw that up. Shawn set her glass back down and walked around the table.

Shawn took deep breaths to soothe last-second nerves as she closed in on the bar. Her heart hammered even harder than before, but she was going to do this. The woman turned as Shawn got closer. She grinned, brought a shot to her lips, and tossed it back, eyes dancing the whole time.

Don't think! Shawn screamed at herself as she slid onto the stool beside her.

"Took you long enough."

Shawn froze, but she couldn't look away. The challenge in the woman's eyes made something unfurl inside her.

"I'm Keisha." The woman held out a hand.

Shawn accepted it, but instead of shaking it, she gripped lightly and let go. "Shawn."

"Drink?" Keisha asked.

"No, I've had enough." Shawn paused, searching for something to say. "I want to be sober enough to enjoy this."

Keisha hummed.

Shawn's sudden sense of relief was damn near overwhelming. It wasn't an awful start. That line was all kinds of smooth. She was amazed it came out of her.

Keisha reached out and closed her hand around a mass of Shawn's dreadlocks. She let the length sift through her fingers. "How long have you been growing those?"

"Seven years. I usually touch them up myself. I don't like people seeing me cry." Maybe this was like riding the proverbial bicycle. Either that or the bartender laced her drinks with something wonky. Was Spanish fly an actual thing?

Chuckling, Keisha leaned closer. "Thanks for the information. I'll try not to pull too hard later."

Goodness. Shawn sucked in a surprised breath. This was really happening. She wasn't sure what to say, so Shawn met her gaze and waited.

As the seconds ticked by, Keisha's eyes dimmed a bit, but she didn't move away. Shawn's stomach sank regardless. She was about to fall off that bike and skin her knee.

Keisha sighed. "So, let me guess. You're one of those butches that has to be in control of everything?"

"Well, that's not stereotypical at all," Shawn answered irritably.

Keisha dragged her gaze from the top of Shawn's head all the way down. When she looked up again, she quirked a brow.

Shawn laughed. She wasn't sure where it came from, but she went with it anyway. She glanced down at her clothes: a sleeveless T-shirt and cargo shorts. "Okay, yeah. I dress the part. Doesn't mean anything."

The light returned to Keisha's eyes. "Is that right?"

"It is. I read. I think, and I feel too," Shawn answered sarcastically. "We already talked about me crying."

Keisha's smile turned into laughter as she pushed her drink away. "I think I want to be sober for this too."

Heat blossomed in Shawn's chest and trickled to the pit of her stomach. Jesus.

They talked, laughed, and every time Keisha touched her, Shawn grew a few inches taller. She'd forgotten how good flirting felt. She'd forgotten what it was like to have a woman focused on her.

"Your friends are getting up. You weren't planning on leaving with them were you?"

Shawn turned slightly to see Veda coming her way. She should probably go. This wasn't her thing. She tried to push away how good this whole night felt…how good this conversation felt.

Keisha yanked on her shirt, and Shawn met her gaze. Keisha pulled her closer and flicked her tongue over Shawn's lips. She didn't expect the flare of arousal, but there it was, curling in her belly.

"I can make you a better offer."

Keisha had Shawn's full attention.

"Come home with me so you can feel how wet I am." Her voice was thick, urgent.

Sweet baby Jesus. Shawn was speechless. What the hell did she do to cause that?

An arm slid over her shoulder. "I'm gonna get an Uber. See you in the morning." Veda was grinning like a proud parent. Brad and Jaime were too. Shawn's mouth opened, but nothing came out. Veda stepped away and staggered toward the door.

Keisha snaked a hand up the inside of her thigh, and Shawn whipped her head back around. Then, Keisha stood and took her hand. "Let's go."

Shawn nodded and followed.

Shawn didn't think it was possible to be a step away from an anxiety attack and aroused at the same time, but she was living, breathing proof that it was. They had barely touched on the way, but Keisha talked a good, filthy game. The kisses they'd shared when they finally stumbled into the living room nearly melted Shawn's face off.

Now, she sat on Keisha's bed and stared at the closed bathroom door. What was she doing? This was a bad idea. It had to be. What if this was some kind of scam and she was about to be robbed? God, what if Keisha was recording this and the video ended up on YouPorn?

Shawn picked at her nails and tapped her foot against the hardwood floor.

Did Keisha expect her to be naked when she came out? Shouldn't she at least take her shoes off and try to look comfortable? What if she didn't like Shawn's technique? What if—? Shawn exhaled noisily and inwardly screamed at the voice in her head.

The bathroom door opened, and Keisha walked out wearing a short, satiny red robe that stopped right at the top of her thighs. It clung to her. Moisture dotted her chest, and thanks to the light behind her, Shawn could see the outline of every curve.

This had to be some kind of YouPorn trap.

Keisha untied the belt to her robe, giving Shawn a tantalizing peek of her full breasts, slightly curved stomach and her neatly shaven sex.

Shawn's mind went blank. Then her thoughts started to whirl.

Keisha smiled and slowly walked toward her. "I meant to mention earlier. I'm recently tested and disease free." Suddenly, she paused and tilted her head to the side. She let out a soft laugh. "You're nervous?"

Shawn swallowed and stared. She'd been with the same woman for the last five years. The possibility of STDs didn't even occur to Shawn. It should have. Her anxiety went up a notch. It was conclusive proof that she had no business doing this, but here she was with a naked woman a few feet away.

"That's so sweet." Keisha started moving again. "You still want me?"

In Shawn's opinion, that wasn't the question that needed to be asked. "Do you...still want me?"

Keisha eased the robe off her shoulders and lowered herself onto Shawn's lap. "Fuck, yes. You're different, and that's so fucking hot."

Shawn's breathing went ragged and loud. She slid her hands around Keisha's waist, up her back and down again until she was palming her ass. Keisha's skin was soft, hot, and slightly damp.

"How long has it been?"

Shawn couldn't believe that they were still talking. "Six months."

"Don't worry. It's not something you forget." Keisha pulled Shawn's hands away from her ass and placed them on her breasts. She arched her back, pressing her hardened nipples into Shawn's palms.

Shawn groaned, and within seconds, she was tweaking, pulling, and then sucking.

Keisha whimpered, and at that moment, Shawn was a giant. All it took was being wanted. It didn't matter that it was probably only for the night.

Their mouths met and breath stuttered between them.

"Fuck me," Keisha whispered.

Shawn knew what to do. Spreading her own legs, she ensured that Keisha's thighs were splayed wide. Shawn grasped Keisha's left hip, lifting her slightly. It gave her just enough room. As she glided into wet heat, Shawn moaned. Immediately, she set the pace, hard and deep.

The breathy keening sounds that fell from Keisha's lips were like little bits of fire that dripped all over Shawn, igniting her in a way she hadn't felt for a long time.

Keisha met her thrust for thrust, and as she promised earlier, she wrapped several dreads in her hand and yanked as she came. Keisha's body quaked, and as she slumped forward, she continued to clutch and pulse around Shawn's fingers.

"Don't stop."

Shawn shivered, pulled Keisha into a kiss, and started again.

Shawn stood on the sidewalk and looked around her. The stretch of Canal looked familiar. Seeing the CVS on the corner helped. Her phone vibrated against her hand for the umpteenth time, but this time Veda was calling instead of texting.

"Yesss."

"You're not answering me."

"I'm trying to get situated." Shawn started walking again.

"You're not gonna be late are you?" Veda sounded alarmed. "It's training, but still."

"No, I'm not. I just figured out where I was."

"So…" Veda dragged the word out.

Shawn smiled. "What?"

"I will cut your hair in your sleep if you play with me."

Shawn chuckled. "She dropped me off downtown. I wasn't comfortable telling her I worked at Stumpy's sex shop."

"I do believe it's called an emporium, but I don't blame you. Stayed the whole night, huh?" Veda's tone was hopeful.

"I did." For the first time in a while, Shawn didn't feel like the gum on the bottom of somebody's shoe. Was it healthy? Probably not, but for now, it worked.

"I'm willing to listen to details if you wanna gush about the whole thing. You know, if I must."

"How gracious." Shawn walked further down the street until she saw pink.

"Isn't it, though?" Veda paused. "No regrets?"

"Not yet."

"I don't know if it was the drinks or the sex, but you sound more relaxed. Feel better?"

"Somewhat."

"Hallelujah. You'll get no slut shaming from me. I'm glad it helped."

Shawn leaned against the building. "Me too."

"Okay. Would you do it again?"

Shawn looked out at the busy street. Life was going full steam ahead around her. "I don't know. She gave me her number and told me to call if I wanted."

"Hmm, it's always good to have options."

She heard the smile in Veda's voice, and Shawn grinned as well. "True. I'd better go, though. I'll see you when I get home."

"I'm going in at nine. I switched with the morning manager for the week. You know what bus to catch to get to our townhouse, right?"

"I do."

"All right, but I expect dinner on the table."

Shawn chuckled. "It's actually your night, but if I have to cook, we're having movie night too."

Veda groaned. "Fiiine, but nothing too gory or scary."

"That's a prerequisite for all horror films."

"Right, how could I forget." Veda voice was full of sarcasm. "Just know, if it keeps me up, you have to stay up with me."

"Deal. I'll see you later."

CHAPTER 3

AFTER HEARING THE DOOR CREAK open, Shawn glanced up at the video feed. A man entered the store. A few minutes later, he gathered an armful of what looked to be cock rings. Confused, Shawn went to the window. Sure enough, the man was walking toward her with quite the load. He only had one cock. Was he going to try to put them all on? That was probably going to be painful, but people had their kinks.

"Hey." The man plopped all the cock rings on the ledge.

"Afternoon." Shawn tried to smile.

"Can you make a recommendation?"

Telling him to grow a vagina because they were much easier to deal with didn't seem like a good idea. Shawn scanned the merchandise and did her best to keep a straight face. "The blue one. It matches your eyes."

The man smiled. He *smiled*. "That's sweet. Thank you."

Shawn nodded.

"I'll put the rest back for you."

He was sweet too. "Thanks!"

Shawn snapped on a pair of gloves and scanned the cock ring.

"I want a token too."

She paused and then nodded. Maybe he really did need to grow a vagina for his own personal use. Shawn gave him his token and change. "Enjoy!" She grinned. She couldn't help it.

He smiled again and walked toward the back.

Shawn watched him. The only bathroom was at the other end of that hallway which was where he was headed. There was no way she was going to use it, ever. She didn't mind the eventual urinary tract infection from holding it in. There was a perfectly clean restroom in the drugstore next door, waiting for her to finish her shift.

A little while later, Shawn decided to have lunch. She opened the microwave, stuck her finger deep into the leftover bowl of pasta, and burned the crap out of herself. "Shit!" She shoved her finger in her mouth and used the bottom of her shirt to carry her food to the little table and chair Phyllis had set up in the office. It really wasn't that bad. Shawn had access to a mini fridge, microwave, Internet, and even porn if she wanted. It was like her own little fortress of solitude. There was a TV too but it had shitty reception.

After her first day alone, she'd learned pretty quickly that if the customers weren't flowing in constantly, working at Stumpy's was boring. She'd been bringing her laptop since. That was a week ago. Since then, she'd been selling vibrators, tokens, and various volumes of *Fuck Me with Power Tools* like crazy. With the help of a customer, Shawn had been educated on the fact that there were ten installments in that series.

The most important thing she'd learned was to keep a pair of latex gloves handy so she didn't have to handle money or tokens post-jerk off. The cock ring guy had been her only customer in hours. Things had been slow, but she was willing to bet most of the real porn connoisseurs were working. Things would pick up soon enough.

Shawn sprinkled a few drops of Napa Valley Habanero hot sauce on her food. The bottle was almost gone, but she had quite a few other sauces in her collection to choose from in the future. She stuck a plastic fork in her pasta, opened her laptop, and clicked on Netflix. Starting *Jessica Jones* was tempting since she was probably the last person in the free world to see it, but it was going to have to wait. The new season of *Wentworth* came first. For shits and giggles, she'd brought *Ringu* and *Audition* from her own horror movie collection, in case Netflix got old. Japanese horror always hit the spot.

Shawn's phone rang. It was much too early for that because it was her day off. She groaned and reached out to blindly search the nightstand.

"'Lo?"

Pink

"Is this Shawnna Green?"

"Yeah, who's this?"

"This is Neil Pastor with Boys and Girls' World. I received your resume a couple weeks ago."

Shawn sat up in bed. "Yes, thank you for the call back."

"Hmm. It says here that you have almost seven years of experience with children."

"That's correct. I worked with them in the home, school, and community."

"I see, and you have a Bachelor in Social Work?"

"Yes. I'm open to getting a Master's but the position said 'either or'." Why was he reading her resume to her?

"Okay, thank you." He hung up.

Shawn took the phone away from her ear and stared at it. "What the hell?" It was probably safe to say that Boys and Girls' World was a lost cause. She shoved her cell phone under the pillow and pulled the covers over her head.

Sometime later, Shawn's pillow started to vibrate and ring. She jolted in surprise and fished her cell from its hiding place. Shawn cleared her throat before she pressed talk. Maybe things would go better if she pretended to be coherent from the start.

"Yes, this is Shawnna Green."

"Hey."

A warmth seeped into her chest. At first, Shawn was relieved to hear Courtney's voice. She was okay. It had been almost two months, and Shawn didn't think she'd ever hear from her again. Some part of her remembered the way they used to be. The way they used to laugh, talk, and do everything together. Those memories brought with them recollection of the fights and the things Courtney had said in blatant attempts to hurt her. Then, it was as if someone had flung her off a mountain. There was no other way to describe the breath-sucking sense of anxiety and impending doom.

"What do you want?" Shawn practically growled the words.

"I just wanted to make sure you were okay."

"I didn't exist for you while you were out fucking around, and now you pretend to be concerned?" Shawn sat up in bed. She gripped her phone hard enough to break it, and her body felt like it was about to come apart. She was trembling.

"You're still angry with me. I guess I can understand that."

"You guess? Are you fucking kidding me?"

"Don't curse at…" Courtney's voice trailed off.

Shawn heard somebody talking in the background. Abruptly, all sound disappeared.

"Hello?"

No answer. Shrinking to nothing was a strange feeling, especially since a week ago she was damn near ten feet tall. The universe had to be laughing at her. Figures Courtney would call when she'd taken some baby steps forward.

"Sorry," Courtney whispered.

"Are you trying to hide me from her? What did you do? Lock yourself in the bathroom?" Shawn stumbled out of bed and stood in the middle of the room.

"I just thought it best that—"

"There is something really wrong with you. You know that?" It was getting hard to breathe. "You're not gonna treat me like I'm nothing. Like I didn't exist. We were out in the open! What you did with her was the goddamn secret!" Shawn's chest heaved.

"You don't want me to call?" Courtney had the nerve to sound hurt.

All of Shawn's other emotions were pushed to the side by sudden indecision. What did she want? Underneath everything, there was a part of her that was happy to hear from Courtney. Wavering on the subject made Shawn even more pathetic.

"I need some kind of contact with you. It doesn't feel right not to," Courtney said.

Shawn's bedroom door opened, and Veda walked in. "I thought I heard you talking. I was getting ready to le—" Veda met Shawn's gaze and didn't finish. "Is that Courtney?"

Shawn wasn't sure how Veda was able to tell who it was. Maybe because her mouth was hanging open and she was floundering like a dying fish.

"Hang up." Veda's tone was firm.

Shawn wanted to. She really did.

Moving quickly, Veda snatched the phone out of Shawn's hand, but the damage was done. It hurt, falling from the high she'd been on.

Veda stared at her. Her face was red, and her lips were pressed together. "Don't let her do this to you. Don't let her pull you down."

Shawn looked away.

"Oh, honey."

"Shawn? Hell—"

Veda ended the call, interrupting whatever else Courtney had to say. Shawn's cell chimed as it was powered down completely.

She closed her eyes. Shawn didn't want to hear the pity in Veda's voice.

Veda sighed. "Truth. This was a setback, but you have to decide if it's gonna be a tiny one or something huge."

If Shawn could sleep, maybe when she woke up, the stinging in her chest would be gone. "V. Give me the phone and go to work."

Veda stepped closer and rubbed a hand down Shawn's back. The touch made her tense up even more but the warmth was still welcome. "You should block her or get your number changed." She set the phone on Shawn's bed.

There were probably a lot of things she should do.

Veda squeezed her arm as she stepped away. "I'll see you later, but I'm here for you. So, if you wanna make little voodoo dolls and burn her ass in effigy, it'll be just between us."

Shawn's eyes burned, but she didn't cry. "I know."

Veda nodded and walked away. A moment later, the front door opened and closed.

Even after Veda left, Shawn still stood in the middle of her room. Grimly, she looked around her. Everything she owned was right in front of her, and it all fit in a couple of boxes. She'd sold all the furniture. It had been secondhand, anyway. She pretty much had nothing except her clothes, computer, an extensive horror movie collection, and an even more extensive hot sauce collection. This was what she'd let herself be reduced to.

Shawn reached for her phone and powered it back on. Then, she searched through her few contacts until she got to Keisha Vance.

Keisha's cries of pleasure were sharp and loud.

Listening to them didn't completely fill the hole Courtney's phone call had left, but it helped. She was in control of this woman's pleasure, and it felt so damn good to be in control of something. It wasn't a butch thing. It was a human thing.

Keisha's back was slick with sweat. Her entire body moved with each downward thrust. Shawn liked the view of her from behind. The play of muscles, her fisted hands holding on to the sheet, the arch of her spine, and the curve of her ass were all things of beauty.

She spread her legs wider, and Shawn went deeper. She watched her latex-covered fingers disappear and appear again, wet and slippery. Steadily and for the third time, Shawn increased the pace, and Keisha was there to meet it.

Leaning forward, Shawn pressed against Keisha, allowing herself to enjoy the skin on skin contact. Shawn's hardened nipples scraped against Keisha's back, making her shiver and moan.

"Oh…fuck," Keisha whimpered brokenly. The smooth rhythm of her hips became jerky, disjointed. Then, her body quivered as she called out, "Fuck!"

Keisha's inner muscles clenched and throbbed, pulling Shawn deeper. She followed, riding out the wave of Keisha's orgasm.

It wasn't enough, and as Keisha's upper body slumped toward the bed, Shawn began pumping, harder, faster than before. The bed squeaked with her efforts.

"God yessss!"

It wasn't long before Keisha came once more.

Keisha hummed and trailed her fingers up Shawn's stomach and around her left breast. "I have to get to work soon, but I'd be happy to do that thing with my tongue—"

Covering Keisha's hand with her own, Shawn squeezed. "Thanks, but not this time." She'd gotten as much satisfaction as she could out of the past couple hours.

"Mmm, too bad." Keisha yawned. "For future reference, I'm not a fan of one-sided sex."

Shawn met Keisha's gaze for a hot second before looking away. "Sorry."

Keisha sat up. "Hey, no. Don't apologize." She sighed. "All of this"—she waved her hand between them—"isn't you, is it? I'm not just talking about the sex. One minute you're confident and then you sort of disappear."

It was a little weird that Keisha was so observant, but it was a relief as well. Shawn exhaled noisily. "No, it really isn't. I'm struggling right now."

Leaning back against the wall, Keisha waited silently for more, but Shawn didn't have the energy to give it to her.

"Okay, I get it. I'm gonna use your shower, then." She got out of the bed and looked at Shawn expectantly.

"Right around the corner. You can't miss it."

Keisha nodded. When she got to the doorway, she stopped and turned. "I'm glad you called me. Hope I was able to help with whatever."

Shawn sat up in the bed and pressed her back against the wall. She smiled softly. "You did."

Maybe tomorrow she'd have it in her to block Courtney's number.

CHAPTER 4

SHAWN'S HEART RACED AND BLOOD rushed in her ears. She could still hear Courtney screaming at her about feeling smothered. The dream was stuck on repeat inside her head. Sitting on the side of the bed, Shawn leaned forward and pressed her hand against her chest, trying to control the blossoming pain. She'd woken up feeling like someone had ripped her open. It had been the same yesterday and the day before that. The past few mornings had been shitty, and she was tired of holding it in. Shawn wanted the good to outweigh the bad. She had a job; she had Veda; and she had a woman who was a phone call away, willing to do anything she wanted. On the other side, there was Courtney and five years of history, and somehow that history and that woman still had a whole lot of power over her.

After several seconds, her heartbeat slowed. Shawn took a couple of breaths to try to relax even more, but parts of her were stuck in those five years, wallowing in the good, the bad, and the ugly. For three and a half of them, things had been perfect with Courtney, at least in Shawn's eyes. Then suddenly, the dependability Shawn had always provided was boring and overbearing, and being understanding wasn't enough anymore. Were there times when she pushed too hard? Yeah, no doubt. Shawn had to relearn a lesson not to shower affection on someone who wasn't feeling the same way. That wasn't even rock bottom. That was when she cried and begged Courtney to stay. That was then and this was now, and in the moment, it was hard to remember who she used to be. Shawn was scared that the woman Veda knew was gone.

The pain in her chest went back to the dull ache she was learning to live with. Maybe she just needed to try harder to pull herself out of this funk. It

Pink

was impossible to throw herself into the crappy job at Stumpy's. There was no sense of accomplishment, no semblance of reward.

Fortunately, Shawn didn't need to be told how cliché it was to find redemption between a woman's thighs. God, it sounded like something from a trashy romance, but she had to admit that the shit was working pretty well for the most part. She expected to feel hollow and dirty, but instead she felt the opposite.

Sure, she slept around a time or six during college, but wasn't that what she was supposed to do? Wasn't that what everybody did? Shawn hadn't felt dirty then either, but had always thought she was too young to know better. Fucking around during freshmen and sophomore year didn't quite have the same effect as it did now. Back then, she was on top of the world: invincible and all-knowing. There was no place to fall, and there was no reason to either. Right now, she was hurting, but she could see some daylight. Maybe that was going to have to do. Little by little, Shawn aimed to whittle away at the dreariness around her until the sun shined full blast.

The welcoming smell of brewing coffee hit her. Pressing the heels of her hands against her eyes, she tried to shake herself out of the haze she'd fallen into. It helped a little, but Shawn figured that a shit-ton of coffee would help even more, especially since it was barely six o'clock in the morning. She grabbed a hair tie from the nightstand and piled her dreads high on the top of her head. Veda had to be up. Sure enough, when Shawn entered the living room, Veda was on the couch, sipping from a huge mug. *The Today Show* was on with the volume low.

"Good morning."

Shawn grunted in response and walked right into the kitchen. After pouring her coffee, she put enough cream in to render it lukewarm before taking a sip.

"You're up early," Shawn said.

With her cup in tow, Shawn ventured back out into the living room and plopped down on the couch beside Veda.

"So are you," Veda replied.

"Yeah, couldn't get back to sleep, so I gave up trying."

Veda stared at her, but Shawn hid part of her face behind the oversized coffee mug.

"What's wrong?"

Shawn shrugged.

"Oh c'mon. You know I need more than that. If I could read minds, I'd be so fucking rich I'd find a way to make the French Quarter smell like potpourri instead of piss."

Shawn cracked a smile, but it fell quickly. "Aren't you tired of hearing about my shit?"

Veda set her cup down on the table and turned to her. "Are you?"

"Yeah, I am."

"Doesn't mean you're not still going through it."

"Yeah, well, I can't wait till I get to the point where I don't feel anything for her." Shawn's entire body sagged under the weight of all the crap.

Veda wrapped an arm around her and Shawn slumped against her. "At least you accept that you need to work on things."

"Mmm, I guess. You know, my life would be a hell of a lot better if we were a thing."

Veda snorted. "A thing, huh? Never mind the fact that I'm straight and not your type. You can barely handle my personality as a friend."

"Pfft, semantics."

"Oh, is that what all that is? Let's not forget that it would have been like fucking my sister, if I had one."

Shawn wrinkled her nose. "Yeah, there is that. You know, there's actually a movie. It's called Sister My—"

"No, I don't wanna know."

"Good, because it's pretty fucked up." Shawn chuckled and sighed. "God, I miss being in college. Messing up was looked over because it was all part of the experience."

"Until it wasn't."

"Losing your scholarship still stings like that?" Shawn asked.

"Sometimes, especially since my mom brings it up at least once a month. Other times, I think it wasn't for me anyway. I'm doing fine. I could have gotten loans, but I pay the government enough as it is."

"She really still digs into you about it?"

"Hell, yes," Veda scoffed.

"My parents tried to give me relationship advice when I finally told them me and Courtney weren't doing well."

"You're kidding. What did they say?"

"Put a ring on it if I wanted to keep her."

Veda pulled away slightly. Her lips trembled and she sputtered with laughter. "I'm sorry."

Shawn rolled her eyes and smiled despite the heaviness she felt. "Worst advice ever. So glad I didn't even think about taking it."

"For real."

"Of course, all that changed when I told them she cheated. Hell, my mom was just as upset as I was. They offered me money to help get started here, but I couldn't take it. I need to do this on my own."

"You still tell them everything, huh?"

"Pretty much."

"They know how hard it's been for you emotionally, I mean?"

Shawn sighed, "Yeah. I made friends, plenty of them, but they were all her people first. It's like I'm starting all over again with the bare bones, you know. You and my parents."

"Nothing wrong with that. Sounds like a strong base to me. It's a positive. It might help if you saw more things that way instead of viewing it as settling."

"I'm trying."

Veda stared.

"I am."

She quirked a brow. "Did you block Courtney's number?"

Okay, well she was working on trying. Shawn reached for her coffee cup and mumbled.

"What? Didn't hear you."

"Not yet. I know I should, but I can't. I doubt she'll call again, and I won't call her. This is my last piece of her. I've got her number and a few pictures left on my phone. I spent five years with her. I can't just cut her out like that."

"You mean like she tried to do you? Used a big-ass butcher knife too."

"I know she did. I'm not her, though."

"No, you're not. You were always too good for her anyway." Veda threw an arm over her shoulder and pulled her close again, leaving Shawn with a solid sense of belonging.

"Yeah, you told me that a time or two."

"A fuck sight more than that." Veda snorted.

"Yeah, a lot more." Shawn sank into her friend's embrace. "When I get to where I need to be, there'll be plenty of cutting, but I'll use an axe."

"There she is." Veda gave her a sloppy kiss on the cheek. "Sun's coming up. You want waffles?"

"Only if it comes with bacon."

"You do the bacon. I'm all over those waffles and forget the hot sauce this morning. It's painful to watch you eat sometimes. Hot sauce on bacon, really?" Veda rolled her eyes.

"Fine, fine." Shawn smiled. The dull ache in her chest had retreated farther. Most of it had to do with the company, and the rest was because Shawn actually made a real effort to push through it.

"Sir, I'm sorry, but that doll is for display purposes only." Shawn stared at the customer and did her best to smile through his belligerence.

"Her name is Debbie! It says so on all the packages. I don't have time to blow her up. Does it look like I have an air pump in my pants?" His face was blotchy red, but all his hair was damn near white, including his beard. Shawn hadn't thought it possible for a person to actually look like a tomato.

"Sir, what you do in your own time is your business." No, she didn't have to go there, but he left himself open for that one. This was getting to be entertaining. It was a plastic woman. What did it matter if it was inflated or not? It would never feel like the real thing. He could wrap the deflated version around his junk a few times and yank. Probably get the same effect.

The man stared. He beat a fist against the counter. "I wanna talk to your supervisor."

"I'm the only one here."

"Well! Get her on the phone!"

The few other people in the store were really starting to pay attention. Weren't things like this better with an audience anyway? Especially since he was the one looking like an ass. "Fine. Let's do that."

This probably wasn't the best idea, but she was in this to win it. No way Phyllis would tell her to practically break her neck trying to reach that thing. Shawn reached for the cordless. Phyllis answered on the second ring.

"Is everything okay?"

Pink

"For the most part, but there's a nice older gentleman here who wants the blow-up doll—"

"Debbie! Her name is Debbie!"

For fuck's sake, someone needed to give her strength. "The blow-up Debbie on display."

"That's fine. You're a tall drink of water. Use the ladder, shouldn't take much. Let him know it'll cost him double."

For a full few seconds, Shawn was speechless. She looked at the white-haired man, and he stared back at her impatiently. "I'll do it for double the price."

He turned even redder. "Fine! I only have twenty minutes left in my break, so hurry up."

Phyllis chuckled. "Excellent. Do you need anything else?"

"No... No, that's all." Shawn hung up. Without another word, she grabbed the ladder and unlocked the door.

Shawn set the ladder right underneath Debbie. Everything around her seemed to come to a standstill. Everyone was staring. Maybe the audience thing wasn't all it was cracked up to be. Shawn cleared her throat and looked up at the doll. How the hell did Phyllis get it to sit in the swing so perfectly? She shook her head and climbed up. Thankfully, she only had to go about halfway. Reaching up, Shawn tugged at Debbie, but she didn't budge. Dust, however, flew all over the place, making her sneeze.

What the hell? She went up another step until she was almost staring into Debbie's gaping crotch. She was obviously always up for some action. Shawn couldn't help herself. She smirked and whispered, "Sorry." Then, she yanked at Debbie once more.

This time, Debbie came along like the good girl she was. A loud whooshing release of air followed.

Debbie had sprung a leak.

"Shit! Quick, give her to me."

Shawn looked down at the white-haired man. He waved at her urgently. She shrugged and dropped Debbie into his arms. She'd lost a bit of oomph already. A few seconds later, Shawn was back on the floor, staring in utter disbelief.

The white-haired man had his mouth wrapped around the back of Debbie's right thigh. Desperately, he tried to replace the air she was losing. So much for not having the time. He mumbled something.

"What?"

He ripped his mouth away. "Tape!" He yelled and went back to pushing life back into Debbie.

Yeah, they had tape. Some of that good electrical kind. Shawn was tempted to make him pay five bucks for a strip of it, but decided that would be too mean. The man was obviously in distress.

"Okay, hold on." A line had formed at the counter. Some of the patrons were gaping while others were smothering their grins.

The white-haired man nodded.

Shawn went back to her little shack. As she grabbed the tape from under the cash register, she told the customers, "Give me just a minute, folks. I'm performing surgery." She snapped on her latex gloves. Hell, she should have had them on the whole time.

One of the customers laughed. Shawn didn't dare look that way or she'd join in.

By the time Shawn got back to the white-haired man, Debbie looked a little wrinkly but doable. There was nothing wrong with a man who worked hard to get what he wanted. Shawn tore a long strip of tape off the roll and gestured for him to lift his head. As quickly as she could, Shawn wrapped the tape around Debbie's thigh.

The man turned and ran toward the back. Shawn didn't get a thank you or anything from him, but over his shoulder, Debbie peered at her with a forever-frozen look of surprise on her face. Shawn smiled. It was genuine and unhurried. The money was shit, but maybe this job wasn't so terrible after all.

CHAPTER 5

"It's staring at me. I don't think I can eat something with eyes." Shawn poked her dinner with her fork.

Veda groaned. "For fuck's sake, turn it around, then, or pull the eyes off. I refuse to let you waste good crawfish."

"Whatever. I can't believe you thought I'd eat this."

"Have you even bothered to taste it? No. You've spent twenty minutes bitching about it."

"It looks like a giant bug!" Shawn held up a large crawfish with her thumb and forefinger and dangled it over her plate.

Veda stared at her from across the table. It was covered in newspaper and on top was a huge bowl filled with crawfish, smoked sausage, corn, and potatoes. "Well that's why they call 'em mudbugs, you ass."

"They got them from the mud?"

"People are starting to stare and now isn't the time for you to play twenty questions," Veda hissed.

Shawn looked up and around. Sure enough, they were.

"Listen. Deanie's is no slouch. It's a well-known spot in Metairie for seafood. Forget about what it is and follow my lead. Try something new."

Sighing, Shawn nodded. She watched as Veda ripped off the crawfish tail and peeled it open. It took her a minute to do it herself, but when she was done, Shawn held a little strip of red-and-white-tinged meat in her fingers. She closed her eyes and popped it in her mouth.

It wasn't bad at all. Spicy, lemony, and salty. "Okay, it's—" Horrified, Shawn watched helplessly as Veda brought the remainder of the crawfish body to her mouth and sucked. "Oh my God! Why are you...? I'm not doing that!"

Veda snorted, and within seconds it became full blown laughter. "The look on your face!"

"Fuck you," Shawn whispered harshly.

Veda laughed even harder and sucked on a claw.

Shawn glared and picked up another crawfish.

"It's the best part. It took me a while to do it. Maybe a year or so, and since we're talking about food, I have to tell you that the best thing to come out of your relationship with Courtney is that you learned to eat something besides cereal, ramen, chicken fingers, and fries."

Shawn grinned because right now it was easy. "I like wings too, but yeah, you're probably right."

"Remember when our microwave broke and you were too lazy to go out in the common area to use that one?"

"I wasn't being lazy. I was too tired to make nice with the prissy girls who hung out there. It was easier to just use the coffee pot. I cleaned it out afterward." Shawn chuckled. "Since we're going down memory lane, I haven't noticed any Doritos in the house. You used to pour hot sauce on them and eat them like a delicacy."

"Oh, I still do that when I'm PMSing. It's the only thing I eat with hot sauce. Some women like chocolate. I like soggy, spicy Doritos, and don't be such a hypocrite. You fucked some of those prissy girls."

"Ugh, don't remind me. I try to forget the pillow princesses. Anyway, you're one to talk. How many times did I open the door to see dick swinging in your face?"

Veda cackled. "You know most of that was unplanned. I didn't have time to warn you."

"Whatever. It takes two seconds to text 'Dick in my mouth. Don't disturb.'"

They glanced at each other and laughed uproariously.

Shawn leaned forward and whispered, "People are staring again."

"Oh, fuck 'em," Veda said between chuckles.

Shawn shook her head.

"What?" Veda asked.

"I feel almost human, you know?"

Veda smiled. "That's a good thing."

Pink

"I know. When we're talking and laughing, when I'm a work, and when I'm fu—"

"Fucking your way to oblivion?" Veda interrupted.

Shawn rolled her eyes. "Yeah, I guess you could say that."

"I did."

"Smart ass," Shawn snarked.

"Uh-huh, since you brought that up, I have a question." Veda leaned forward.

"Okaaaay."

"Keep in mind I'm trying to help, but with your emotions all over the place, is it the best idea to keep seeing *just* Keisha?"

"What do you mean *just* Keisha?" Needing something to do with her hands, Shawn started tearing away the label on her beer.

Veda narrowed her eyes. "I think you have an idea what I'm about to say."

"Say it, then."

"I was going to whether you liked it or not. The more you sleep with her, the more chance there is of developing feelings. From what you told me, she's not new to the game, so she knows how to handle herself. You, on the other hand, haven't done this for a long time. You could end up getting hurt or in some messy rebound relationship that doesn't work out."

Shawn sighed and looked heavenward. When she glanced down again, there was a nice pile of shredded paper in front of her. It was safe to say her nerves were a little wracked. "We're having fun, and she makes me feel—"

"I know what she makes you feel."

"She's cool people, and I'm not trying to get my emotions caught up in this."

"I know that too. All I'm saying is there's nothing wrong with what you're doing, but—"

"Good, because I'm not stopping. I'm gonna see her."

Veda pursed her lips. "Will you let me finish? God!"

Shawn held up a placating hand. "All right, sorry."

"Thank you. Now, hear me out. The more active you are, the less time you have to wallow. Why don't you look around a little? Date, fuck around, and maybe make some friends."

Shawn's whole body tensed. "I like Keisha. I'm comfortable with her."

"And that's the problem. That's why that situation is dangerous for you emotionally. If you were seeing other women too, there's a chance to balance things out."

"Is that supposed to make sense? Juggling more than one woman is supposed to balance things out?" Shawn asked.

"You're not listening. There's nothing to juggle. You're gonna be open about what you want. You said keeping it casual was working for you."

"It was. It is. I don't know if I'm ready for something like that. I—"

"Hold on." Veda raised her hand as she interrupted. "I said have some fun. There's plenty of women out there like Keisha. There isn't a damn thing wrong with a woman taking charge of her own pleasure. Let's make a profile for you on Tinder, and you could be upfront about what you want. Women appreciate that, I hear."

While she let Veda's words soak in, Shawn stared. "I'm not nineteen anymore. I'm thirty-one."

"What the hell does that have to do with anything?"

"I don't know. It just sounded good," Shawn said sheepishly.

Veda glared.

"I can't believe you're encouraging me to do this."

"It's not a matter of encouraging. If it's working for you, let it. Hell, I've done it. Men do it all the time, but you get to be more honest about it. I'm pretty sure Keisha wouldn't mind."

"No, she knows what we're doing. And she's seeing other women besides me anyway." Shawn shrugged. At least Keisha was discreet about it. Helped give Shawn some peace of mind.

"Well, there you go."

Shawn crossed her arms over her chest. "I'm too old for this shit."

Veda snorted. "That sounded better than what you said earlier, but is it because you really believe that? Or are you buying into the slut shaming society tries to push on women and the gay community as a whole?"

A little taken aback by the complexity of Veda's question, Shawn blinked. "What?"

"Oh, you heard me. Do what you wanna do. We should all do what feels good every once in a while, and fuck what people say about it."

Shawn smirked. "Now that sounded more like you."

Veda glared again. It was a little more intense this time. "Keep on. I'm serious one day you're gonna wake up bald. I'll take it all and throw it out for the possums. Don't be surprised if you see one of them wearing your dreads like a hat when you go take out the garbage."

"You're not right in the head. You know that?"

"Yes, this I know."

"I'll think about the Tinder thing."

"Good."

After taking a long swig of beer, Shawn reached for a potato and popped it into her mouth. As one conversation ended, they launched into another. By the time they got on the bus, it was nearly dark.

"That was a well-spent Saturday afternoon."

Instead of answering, Shawn smiled.

Keisha flopped back onto Shawn's bed, breathing loud and ragged, body covered in sweat. "Damn, phew. That ex of yours—let's call her Dumb Ass—really screwed up when she let you go." She fanned herself and turned over to look at Shawn. "If you fucked her anything like you do me…"

Shawn took Keisha's words as a compliment. Heat flooded her face as she sat up in bed, still trying to catch her own breath. She wasn't sure why she told Keisha about Courtney, but she didn't regret it. Laughing, Keisha reached up and pressed a finger against Shawn's cheek. "Are you blushing? It's hard to tell, but there's this look on your face."

Shawn sucked in a breath. "What? No!"

"You are. God, I don't think they make them like you anymore."

"I'm afraid to ask what that means."

"Nothing bad. Trust me. I'm about to make a blanket statement about butches, at least about the ones around here."

Shawn eyed her warily. "I'm not from here."

"Exactly."

"So, in other words, what you're about to say will get sucked into the universe and add to the stereotype?"

Keisha glared.

Shawn smiled.

"Admittedly, yes, but you're sweet. You listen, and most of all, with us being just fuck buddies, you don't do the cool, aloof thing, which makes you even fucking hotter."

Shawn rolled her eyes. "Oh, stop."

"I'm serious!" Keisha sat up beside her. Their shoulders brushed.

"Well, thank you."

"Welcome. Despite everything that happened, Dumb Ass has to be kicking herself."

Shawn laughed, but there was no humor in it. She tried to swallow down a surge of emotions that included anger, sadness, and guilt, along with acid that was trying to creep up the back of her throat. What the hell did she have to feel guilty about? No matter what their problems were, she wasn't the one who cheated. "I doubt that." The words came out husky, thick.

Keisha leaned into Shawn. "I'm sorry. I didn't mean to kill your mood."

"It's not dead yet. I hate that she has the ability to dampen it, though."

"Well, you're giving it to her."

Shawn met Keisha's gaze. It was true. "Yeah—"

Keisha covered Shawn's mouth with her hand. "Nope, no more talk about that dumb ass. Let's talk about *my* ass, and what you're going to do to it. You're not leaving my house with bad shit on your brain." She sucked Shawn's bottom lip into her mouth. "The only thing on your mind should be the next time."

"Mmm." Shawn pulled Keisha onto her lap. "Is that right?"

Skin met skin. Keisha shivered. "Shut up. Too much talking."

Shawn agreed. There was too much thinking, too.

Rolling her eyes, Shawn typed Tinder into her browser search bar. Then, she promptly went back to other tabs to continue skimming for new jobs on Craigslist, Indeed, and four other sites. There were only a couple of new listings added to the slew she'd already applied for. Her attention wandered again within seconds, so she clicked on the Tinder tab only to see it wasn't an actual website but encouragement to get the app in Google Play or the Apple store.

Pink

"Well, that's how out of touch I am."

She closed the tab and picked up her phone. Over a week had passed since Veda broached the subject, and she hadn't brought it up again. That wasn't Veda's way. Shawn downloaded the app and followed the prompts. Before she knew it, she'd completed her profile. If someone was interested, she'd know soon.

Shawn leaned back in her chair. It was 8:17 a.m. and all was quiet at Stumpy's. She didn't like that too much. Sometimes, she didn't want to think. Today might end up being that way. Shawn stood abruptly. She could check the inventory. At least, out there on the floor, she could hear the moans and cries coming from the back, thanks to the videos on constant rotation. Nothing quiet about that, or maybe being in her own head wasn't such a bad place to be after all.

Some good shit went on in her mind too, and even though sometimes the good emotions got wound up in the shitty stuff, they still existed. Despite her night with Keisha, Shawn wasn't feeling too light *or* too heavy. She was somewhere in between, which was fine.

As a person, there was nothing bad about her, either. Keisha told her so. Veda said it constantly, and so did Shawn's parents. She knew it was true. She *knew* it, but it was like that knowledge was trapped in some reinforced bubble just out of reach. It was getting closer, and there were days when she could actually touch it. Those days had been happening more often the past couple weeks.

Shawn's phone rang, and she was close enough to see that it was Veda calling. "Morning."

"Hey. I don't know if Keisha feeds you, but in case she doesn't, I have a BLT with your name on it if you want?"

"She usually sandwiches me or something, but I stopped and got breakfast from the diner on the corner before coming in. I can eat the BLT for lunch, though. Where are you?"

"About to get off the bus, I'll see you in a minute. I can walk the rest of the way to work."

As the door opened, Shawn looked up at the camera feed. Decked out in her Taco Bell uniform, Veda walked in. Shawn unlocked the office and moved back to let her in.

39

Veda glanced at her and smirked. "At least you're bringing a change of clothes now."

Shawn huffed. "I take a shower too. You think I walk around all day with her all over me?"

Veda's eyes twinkled with amusement. "You said it. I didn't. But that's good to know."

Egged on by her friend's sarcasm, Shawn mumbled, "Whatever. It's a butch stereotype thingy."

"Uh-huh." Veda grinned. "Thanks for sharing. Want your sandwich?" She held up a brown paper bag.

Shawn snatched it.

"I put a Little Debbie in there too."

"Oatmeal cream pie?"

"Didn't you have one of those already?"

"Shut. Up." Shawn swatted at Veda.

Veda laughed and danced out of the way. "Sorry, couldn't help it, but no. We're out. I gave you a Nutty Bar."

"That'll work." Shawn crossed her arms over her chest. "So, why are you doing this?"

"What? I can be sweet." Veda's eyebrows shot up on her forehead. She almost looked affronted.

Shawn snorted and stared.

"I can!" After a few more seconds, Veda threw her hands up. "Fine. I know you're a grown woman and everything, but you're my best friend. No one's taking care of you anymore, so until somebody good enough comes along, I'm in."

A bolt of warmth shot through her. Shawn smiled. "That's sweet, but I don't—"

"Bullshit. Everybody wants or needs that every once in a while. Don't make a big deal out of it. Eat the fucking sandwich and think of me." Veda put a hand on her hip and waited.

Shawn laughed. It was still sweet in a very Veda way. "Okay, I got it."

"Good."

"I got some good news," Shawn said.

"Really? Do tell."

"I did the Tinder thing."

Veda grinned. "Good girl."

Shawn rolled her eyes. Then, she heard the front door open and looked up at the security feed. It was just some guy. She walked back toward the glass so she could keep an eye on him.

"Look at you, taking this job all seriously. It grows on you. It's like people watching, in a way, or looking out at some social experiment."

"Yeah, it is interesting."

The man glanced up at Shawn and started walking her way. When he got close to the window, Shawn asked, "Can I help you?"

The man nodded then smiled. He was clean cut and smooth shaven.

Seconds passed, but he didn't say anything.

Shawn threw Veda a look, but only got a shrug in return.

"Sir, can I help you?"

Mr. Smooth stepped closer and licked his lips. He flashed a wad of money before shoving some in the slot.

"That's twenty-five dollars. You can have it if the two of you kiss for me."

Was this the fucking Twilight Zone? Did men really think money would get them everything they wanted? For twenty-five dollars? That was an insult. Shawn peered at Veda and assumed she'd find her looking as offended as Shawn felt.

Instead, Veda had a thoughtful expression on her face. Her gaze swung from Shawn to the man and back again. She stepped forward. "Make it an even thirty."

Shawn's mouth fell open in shock.

Mr. Smooth's smile was wide and toothy. He nodded as he pulled out another five and slid it under the window next to the rest of the cash. Veda reached past her and took the money. She glanced at Shawn and rolled her eyes. "For fuck's sake, calm down."

Veda smiled at Mr. Smooth, and without another word, turned toward Shawn, yanked her forward, and pressed her pink lips against Shawn's cheek.

A second later, Veda shoved the money into her bra.

"Hey!" Mr. Smooth sounded irate. "What the hell was that?"

Shawn blinked.

Veda grinned wickedly. "I need to go. I'm probably already late. I'll get more oatmeal cream pies and possibly steak. You feel like steak?"

Shawn blinked again.

"I'm gonna take that as a yes. Come lock up after me."

Moving on autopilot, Shawn did what she was told. She expected to see Mr. Smooth at the door, but apparently, he was too shocked to bother. A few seconds later, Veda was gone. Shawn went back to the window and smiled at Mr. Smooth.

He sneered at her.

She shrugged.

"Give me a damn token." He pulled out another five.

After sliding her laptop back in its bag, Shawn had nothing left to do but wait for the cashier from the next shift to relieve her. She really hoped he wasn't going to be late, because she'd have to wait another hour for the bus if that happened. Shawn'd had enough strange for the day, and hanging out at the bus stop meant things could get stranger. She was all for Southern hospitality, but of the New Orleanians she'd met at the RTA bus stops over the past few weeks, Shawn knew who was getting a divorce, who was cheating, and who was stealing burgers from Burger King. That wasn't even the tip of the iceberg. She knew life stories even though she didn't know their names. It wasn't a bad thing, just different, and Shawn was still trying to get used to it.

Her cell phone rang. It was a number she didn't recognize, but Shawn answered it anyway because it was a local call. "Hello? This is Shawn."

"Shawnna Green?"

"Yes, can I help you?"

"Good afternoon, my name is Amy Shepard. I'm the assistant director at Wonder Haven. Are you still interested in the case management position?"

Shawn was tempted to dance a little jig, or at least the cabbage patch. "I am."

"Good. I have an opening for an interview next Tuesday at ten a.m. Is that good for you?"

"I can make it work."

"Great. Let me give you the address."

Pink

Shawn scribbled it down. "Is that part of St. Charles in the Garden District?"

"It is. We're on the bus and streetcar line. I'm looking forward to meeting you. You have an impressive resume."

"Thank you. Same here." She hung up and started to dance.

Shawn was so caught up in the news, she didn't hear the door open. It wasn't until Stan, the cashier for the next shift, cleared his throat that she stopped and looked up.

He stared.

She waved.

By the time Shawn got to the bus stop, she was sucking wind. She wasn't sure if the crowd was a new batch of folks for the 5:15 or people hoping the 4:15 hadn't come yet. She scanned the faces until she saw a woman in a Burger King uniform. She clutched her bag—no doubt stuffed with cheeseburgers—to her side. Shawn parted the crowd and sat on the wrought iron bench beside her while everyone else leaned over the curb to look for the bus.

"It's late today?" Shawn asked.

"Yeah, doubt it came early. I been here since fo."

Shawn nodded. She gave her the once-over in an attempt to find a name tag, but the woman didn't have one. The lady glanced down at her phone and started typing furiously and shaking her head at the same time.

"I got me some ungrateful-ass kids. They say they tired of burgers. They want chicken sandwiches dis time." She gave Shawn a look of outrage. "Can you believe dis shit?"

Shawn smiled. "They're kids. Some of them don't care how they get what they want. They just want it."

The woman snorted. "Got that right. You got kids?"

"Nope, I work with them."

She turned toward Shawn and gave her an up and down look. "You ain't gotta lie. I seen you come out of Stumpy's. Shit, a job is a job."

"Oh, I work there right now." Shawn wasn't ashamed at all. "I have a job interview at a group home next week."

"Good on you."

Shawn smiled. Yeah, good on her.

43

CHAPTER 6

As she shuffled out of her bedroom, Shawn yawned and stretched for the tenth time. She glanced at the bathroom. The shower was calling her, but the idea of coffee was making her its bitch. They really needed to get a coffee maker with a timer so all the work could be done the night before when one of them was lucid. Shawn stepped toward the living room and paused. The television was on but muted. The thing that caught her eye the most was the naked man sitting on the couch eating cereal.

They blinked at each other.

Moving quickly, he pressed the bowl between his legs.

That bowl needed to be sanitized with alcohol, or better yet, Shawn was going to make sure it got thrown away. She had a million questions running through her head but settled on one to start with. "Why?" Shawn dragged the word out.

"Uh, sorry? Didn't know she had a roommate."

"That's not leather and you're naked. You know that right?"

"I'm Paul, by the way." He held out a hand but kept the bowl against his junk.

She wasn't shaking his hand. Shawn had no idea where it had been the past few minutes. "And you have one of our bowls against your…manly bits. I have to ask again. Why?"

"Um, I was hungry? Thought I'd have a snack before hitting the shower."

So, that meant his dirty, sweaty ass was raking against the cloth couch. They were going to need way more than Febreze for that cushion. Burn it. Burn it with fire. Shawn stared at him. "None of that feels wrong to you?"

Paul's expression screamed helplessness. He blinked owlishly, and his mouth was hanging open.

Shawn waited for an answer. She *needed* an answer. In the periphery, she saw Veda coming down the stairs. She stopped and looked from the houseguest to her roommate.

Paul smiled. He looked relieved. Did he think he was being saved?

"Why is your naked ass on my couch?" Veda asked. The irritation in her voice was obvious.

He lifted the bowl as explanation.

Shawn turned the other way.

"Jesus Christ! Put that away!" Veda screeched.

Thinking it was safe, Shawn turned back. Paul had thankfully covered himself again, but he looked so lost.

Veda sighed. "You have an interview in three hours. Hit the shower. I'll make coffee to get your head in the game and take care of this"—she waved her hand in Paul's direction—"situation."

Shawn nodded, smirked, and headed toward her bathroom.

"Sorry," Paul mumbled, but it was loud enough for Shawn to hear.

"It didn't cross your mind that doing that was nasty?"

Paul didn't say anything.

"Keep the nasty part in the bed—"

Shawn covered her ears. She so didn't want to hear Veda finish that sentence.

After stepping out of the Uber, Shawn's nerves returned in full force. It was like the butterflies in her stomach were bowling. This was her first professional interview in four years. Stumpy's didn't count. She really missed some of her former co-workers and was going to make a point to call them soon. First, she had to jump this hurdle. Shawn had never been good at selling herself, but that was going to have to change on the fly. She needed this job.

Shawn plucked at her shirt. It was a nice shirt and only slightly wrinkled. If she'd taken the bus, that would have been a whole different story. Sitting for an hour and a half and walking from the bus stop would have left her sweaty and unpresentable. Score one for Veda. It had been hard to accept the money for the Uber, but Shawn did. Like some tourist, she kept her gaze glued to the changing scenery that went from the interstate to Uptown to the Garden District. Everything was shiny and picturesque, like a postcard. The houses were huge and opulent with well-manicured lawns and colorful gardens. It screamed old South and money, which made her slightly uncomfortable. She hoped she didn't stick out like a bruised, sore thumb. It wouldn't be the first time that had happened, but it had been a while.

Recalling all that made the butterflies do the goddamn running man. Slowly, Shawn moved up the walkway. She took a couple of deep breaths and reminded herself that she wasn't that depressed person with the self-esteem of a slug anymore. At least, she was trying not to be. Shawn took a few more steps to center herself and decided to fake it until she made it. They didn't know her, so how would they tell the difference?

Wonder Haven looked more like some rich guy's house than a residential home. It had columns, for Christ's sake. Yeah, she probably stuck out. Shawn sighed and pasted a smile on her face. She might as well practice.

A few minutes later, Shawn sat outside the assistant director's office, waiting with her assistant, who was named Janice, along with two other women, and a man who was sweating his ass off even with the air conditioning blowing. Shawn guessed he probably took the bus.

Shawn took the time to study her obvious competition. One woman, the blonde, was biting her nails and staring at her phone. The other woman, a brunette, was looking right at her from behind her glasses. Her green gaze held challenge. Embarrassed, Shawn lowered her eyes but glanced back at her a few seconds later. The woman had taken out her phone as well. That's when it hit her. Were they all early or something?

Janice stood. "Okay, first phase of the interview is the personality test. You'll all be put in separate rooms for privacy, and you'll have thirty minutes to complete the test. If you pass, you'll go on to the final phase, the group interview."

Shawn groaned inwardly. Already, she didn't like this place. Personality test? What New Age crap was this?

The personality test was that Meyer-Briggs crap, which didn't bode well for Wonder Haven in her opinion. Everyone who worked in health care should've known by now it wasn't reliable. Shawn was stuck in a constant eye roll throughout the whole process.

Pink

Almost forty-five minutes later, Janice led her to a conference room where the blonde woman and sweaty guy were waiting along with three perky, perfect-looking people dressed in Wonder Haven polos and khakis. It was all very Stepford-like. Well, at least Shawn knew none of the interviewees were serial killers…yet. That little factoid may have been dependent on who got the job. After all, the whole Stepford thing was contagious. The brunette was missing. Shawn couldn't decide if the woman was a sociopath or a victim of Wonder Haven. They probably had some sacrificial pyre hidden in the backyard or the attic.

When Shawn finally stumbled into an Uber, it seemed like hours had passed. After fishing out her phone, she immediately called Veda.

"So? Did you leave with a good feeling?"

"No, the fuck I didn't! The whole interview was like the *Price is Right* without the buzzer."

"No…really?" Veda's voice went up an octave.

"Yes, really, and there was no Steve Harvey to at least make it entertaining."

Veda chuckled. "I bet Stumpy's is looking real good to you right now."

"Damn right it is." Shawn leaned back and tried to get comfortable. The interior of the car smelled like spicy food, and the backseat had enough stains to be worrisome. This guy was getting three stars, max. Shawn pushed it all away.

"Well, at least it keeps you on your toes in a whole different way."

"Yeah, it's good wholesome entertainment. A real slice of Americana." Shawn pressed the phone to her ear.

Veda snorted.

"So, speaking of entertainment. Did you burn that cushion?"

"You're so funny. Gotta be honest, though. I did Febreze the shit out of it after he left. I didn't want to do it in his face and hurt his feelings."

Shawn cringed. "That's not too wussy for you?"

"He does what I tell him, when I tell him. Sometimes that's all I need."

"Well, it's your party."

"Yeah, and I'll fuck how I want to."

Shawn chuckled.

"Anyway, your next interview is gonna be cake. You got your weird one out of the way."

"That's a thing?" Shawn peered around the inside of the car again. She could definitely believe it was a thing. Weirdness and all.

"It is."

"Lovely."

"Mmm, just to let you know, the assistant manager on the day shift quit, so I'm gonna take it over. We can hang out more often." Veda's voice went in and out as if she was shifting the phone around, but she was still understood.

"Good. I'm so okay with that."

"All right. I better go. This place might fall apart without me."

Shawn was sure she would too. "See you tonight then."

Buck naked and oblivious, Keisha bent over and searched through her purse. She pulled out a clear plastic bag that had two small bottles inside it.

Shawn's attention shifted from her body to the bag. "Wait. Is that…? You carry around your own body wash?"

Keisha shrugged. "Well, yeah. For emergencies."

"Emergency fucks?"

"Something like that." Keisha grinned. "This is only the second time I've been here. I didn't want to walk around all day smelling like you. No offense."

Maybe she would shower with her. Pushing the covers off her lap, Shawn got out of bed. "None taken." She smiled back.

Keisha walked toward her. She yanked softly on dreadlocks that had escaped Shawn's ponytail.

"Good. I'd hate to mess up a good thing by shooting my mouth off. You're good people. I don't have enough of them in my life."

"I could say the same about you, but for the sake of full transparency, I created a Tinder profile."

"And?" Keisha's forehead scrunched. "I have one too."

Shawn started to feel stupid. This wasn't a big deal. Why make it into one? Keisha knew her story, but Shawn couldn't help but wonder what Keisha's was. She hadn't asked and Keisha hadn't volunteered. Maybe she didn't have anything to tell.

Smirking, Keisha inched closer. "You're cute. Did you think it would hurt my feelings?" There was laughter in her voice.

Shawn looked everywhere else around the room instead of at the woman standing in front of her. Keisha kissed her on the chin.

"Don't worry about me, but if you think you need to take a break—"

"No, I'm good. No worries. I mean, I like you. I don't want this to turn into something it shouldn't be." The words rolled quickly off Shawn's tongue.

"Ahh, gotcha, and I agree. I'm not about hurting other women."

"I get that about you."

For several seconds, Keisha stared at her quietly, but her expression was difficult to read. "Soooo been on any 'dates' yet?" She made claw marks in the air for emphasis.

"Not really. I got a couple notifications that someone liked my profile, but I haven't gone further than that."

"Why? Look at you. You're all cheekbones, sexy eyes, and you have that handsome butch thing going for you. Plus, you're sweet and know how to treat a woman, even if it's only for a few hours."

Shawn met Keisha's gaze briefly before looking away. Her words were still hard to believe.

After making a cooing noise, Keisha kissed her chin again. Slowly, her lips trailed upward until they brushed Shawn's. "If I keep coming back, it's good," she whispered. "You're good."

A tingle shimmied its way down Shawn's back. She wrapped her arms around Keisha, pulling her closer. She was excellent for her ego.

Keisha made a sound in the back of her throat and rolled her eyes as she swiped left several times.

"You didn't even look at them," Shawn interrupted.

"I saw enough. Trust me."

They were freshly showered, fully clothed, and sitting on the couch.

"I don't want to make you later for work than you already are."

Keisha glanced up at her and stared.

Shawn smiled.

"If you're going to do this, do it, but you have to know what to look for. Besides, I own the place. They can do without me for a few more minutes. My next hair appointment isn't for another hour. I just like to be prepared." Keisha's purse was over her shoulder, ready to go.

She swiped left a few more times then stopped. "Stay away from this woman right here."

Shawn peered at the profile. "Why? She seems all right."

"Way too much cray for what you're looking for." Keisha went silent. "Her too. She has a weird thing for peanut butter."

"You're kidding?" Shawn laughed.

"Nope. I'm not one to enjoy Peter Pan inside me."

Shawn laughed even harder, and Keisha joined in.

Smiling softly, Keisha asked, "You know something?"

"What?"

"When we get tired of wrecking each other, I think we'll make good friends."

"I can get with that." Shawn smiled in return. Friendship, yeah. She could handle that, and she wanted it too.

Keisha went back to swiping. "Oh…her."

Shawn read the profile out loud, "Make me laugh. Make me feel, make me want you, and I'll do the same. No strings, no crazy, and no drama."

"Damn," Keisha whispered.

"Yeah." Shawn slid the picture down again. The woman, Carmen, a restaurant manager, had vivid blue eyes and jet black hair that tumbled over her shoulders. She was smiling slightly and leaning against the wall. Beside her was a huge painting, alive with a violent slash of red, blue, and orange. She looked to be a woman way out of Shawn's league. "I don't know."

Keisha pressed her finger against the star, indicating a super like. "Too late. Look at it as a challenge. We all need one of those every once in a while. Makes you feel like a fucking queen."

Their gazes met. Keisha cocked a brow.

Shawn blinked. "I'll think about it." Then it hit her. "Is this not weird? Us doing this?" It didn't really feel that way, but it seemed like some sort of odd breach of fuck buddy protocol that she didn't know about.

Keisha smirked. "You mean your present fuck helping you look for another one?"

Pink

"Uh, yeah that."

"I'm a progressive thinker." Keisha stood. Her eyes twinkled with amusement, but there was heat present as well. "If she's the right fit, I wouldn't be opposed to joining in."

Have mercy.

She was serious, too.

Shawn shook her head and grinned as Keisha left. That woman was... well, she wasn't sure, but she was definitely something.

CHAPTER 7

Shawn leaned back in the office chair. It groaned in protest, and so did she as she stretched, pushing her arms way above her head. Stumpy's had been very quiet so far this morning, and Shawn was at the point where she'd give her eye teeth for someone to come in and shake things up. She wasn't sure when it happened, but somehow this job went from necessary to interesting and comfortable. It fit her more than she thought it would, and that sense of belonging was something she needed right now. Watching *It Follows* provided a little distraction. However, she'd seen it several times already. The movie was brilliant, but it didn't hold her attention like it used to.

The door creaked loudly. Shawn glanced up at the security feed. The man who entered was a daily visitor. She didn't know his name, but he was always courteous. She stood up. When she got to the register, Shawn pulled on gloves and grabbed a token as he slid five bucks in the slot.

"Mornin'." The man's smile was big and welcoming.

"Good morning." Shawn grinned in return.

A fine sheen of sweat dotted his forehead. He wiped at it. "I swear to God. I'll never git used to this heat. I've only been in New Awlins since April. Ifin' it gits any hotter, I'm gone turn into a puddle."

"I know what you mean. I'm new to the city too."

"It's nice ta know somebody feels my pain."

Shawn smirked.

The man leaned in. "You know that other place like this a couple blocks down?"

She didn't, but Shawn nodded anyway.

Pink

"They don't even have air conditionin', just some ceilin' fans. Can you believe that? It's so hot, it feels like a dog is breathin' on my balls."

"That's bad?" Shawn asked. Knowledge was power after all, and she was trying to be friendly. He seemed genuine, despite the subject matter of their conversation.

"Hell, yeah. If my sac is sweatin', nothin' on me is comfortable."

"Well, we got plenty of AC."

"Yep, this place is classy." He smiled at her again, showing teeth and all. The man reached into his pocket and then slid a ten in the slot. He nodded and turned away.

Shawn took the ten and shoved it in the pocket of her cargo shorts. She'd been getting a lot of tips lately, mainly from the regulars. Since she'd been working at Stumpy's for months, Shawn was probably considered a regular of sorts too.

After sitting back down, Shawn clicked play on the movie. Her phone chimed. She glanced at it, expecting an email notification. It was from Tinder instead, informing her that Carmen had liked her back. She picked up her cell and stared at it until it went dark again. Shawn's heartbeat doubled. She pressed the home button to illuminate the screen once more.

Sure enough, the notification was still there.

This situation was different than the one with Keisha. Shawn swallowed. Hell, Keisha pretty much pursued her even though she'd been on board every step of the way. Shawn was on her own with Carmen, and she wasn't sure she had the confidence needed to succeed.

Veda had been right. She was getting too comfortable with Keisha. Maybe if she didn't go to Keisha as much, things would fizzle out between them.

So.

She was either going to do this or she wasn't. There was no in between. Shawn took a deep breath. It didn't help anything, but she did it again anyway. All she had to do was send a message. A few words, and Carmen would either respond or not.

Acceptance or rejection.

Keisha said she needed a challenge. Maybe she did. Maybe being with Carmen would help fill in the fissures still inside her. God, a therapist would have a field day with her, but if there was anything she had learned from working in the mental health field, it was that individuals coped in different ways. Shawn wasn't the wreck she was when she first got to New Orleans thanks to Veda and Keisha. Shit, thanks to Stumpy's too.

Acceptance. Rejection.

They were both concepts she had to get used to. It was a chance she had to learn to take again. Shawn clicked the home button on her phone again and opened Tinder. She peered at Carmen's profile, pondering the words, and before she could talk herself out of it, she started typing.

I want you to laugh. I want you to feel. I want you…period.

On her next breath, she sent the message. As if it were on fire, Shawn dropped her phone on the table.

Ding.

"Holy shit." Her breath stuttered in her chest. Shawn stared at her phone like it was going to sprout legs and walk.

The knock on the office window nearly sent Shawn out of her skin. Her heart beat in triple time. When she got to the window, the ten-dollar tipper was smiling. Shawn did her best to emulate it. She must have succeeded.

"Have a good one." He waved.

"Uh, you too."

Seconds later, he was gone.

Shawn made a beeline toward her phone. She had to know what it said. She pushed her fear aside and read Carmen's message. "Holy shit!" Shawn sank back down into the chair. She wasn't seeing things. The words were there as big as day.

Show me.

The sentence was followed by a phone number. Immediately, Shawn's mind gravitated toward the negative. What kind of person gives her number out like that? Shawn wasn't concerned about YouPorn this time, but what if this was some other type of setup? People got robbed doing this shit. People got catfished too.

Somehow, she was able to bring her thoughts to a halt. Tinder was a hookup app. All the people on it took a chance every day. Shawn had decided to be one of them. What a mess. She used to be a whole lot more decisive. Hell, she used to be a whole lot more of everything. She wasn't sure if the old Shawn would do this, but the new Shawn, a combination of who she was then and who she needed to be now, was damn well going to.

Instead of calling, Shawn sent a text introducing herself. Immediately, she decided to be up front about her job. At this point, Keisha even knew. So if Carmen wanted to laugh, Shawn had some Stumpy's stories that she could tell. Her adventures with Debbie was a good start.

LMAO ur making this up.

Nope. True story. Shawn grinned as she typed.

You could write a book.

Don't give me any ideas. I just might. I'd change the names to protect the innocent.

LOL I don't think innocent people come to a sex shop, Carmen wrote.

It's a sex EMPORIUM, Shawn corrected.

My mistake.

You're forgiven. Shawn leaned back in the chair and waited for a response.

Her phone rang.

It was Carmen's number.

Sweet God. Shawn had to scream at herself not to think. She accepted the call. "Hello?"

"I haven't done anything really bad yet. Save your forgiveness."

Shawn melted. Carmen's voice was raspy, but not too deep. It was the kind of voice she wanted whispering in her ear. Shawn pooled every ounce of confidence she'd gained so far. "What does really bad look like on you?"

"That depends on you."

"Meaning?" Shawn swallowed, hard.

"On if you know what you're doing."

For a moment, Shawn faltered. She pushed thoughts of Courtney to the back of her mind. She had no business making an appearance anyway, but there was Keisha, who always seemed satisfied. "I do."

"Mmm, let's get a drink tonight and see where it goes from there."

"Sounds good."

A few minutes later, Shawn ended the call, but she didn't put her phone down. Within seconds, she was texting.

Drinks with Carmen tonight!

It took several minutes for Keisha to respond. She sent a ton of emojis consisting of clapping hands and thumbs up.

I feel like we need to have cake later this week to celebrate.

Shawn chuckled and typed. Red velvet?

Sexy. Let me know when ur free.

I will.

The door creaked open. A redheaded man entered. He was another regular.

When her cell said the Uber, again courtesy of Veda, was six minutes away, Shawn jumped up from the couch and peeked out the window like somehow the car was going to materialize with her name written on the hood.

"Will. You. Stop."

Shawn whipped her head around to stare at Veda.

"What?" Shawn heard her say something, but she wasn't sure of what it was.

Veda sighed and rose from the loveseat. "If you got this far, you're in. Anyway, didn't you do your freak-out already?"

Shrugging, Shawn glanced away and back out the window. Yeah, she already dealt with a horrendous amount of nerves earlier, but this was different. She was anxious, yes, but it had more to do with anticipation than anything. The possibility of being with Carmen represented a lot of things. It meant that Shawn had taken another step to put herself out there, even if it was only a potential hookup. It meant that despite her anger, resentment, and dip in confidence, she was showing that she could function independent of those emotions, independent of Courtney.

The Uber was three minutes away. Shawn pulled the curtain back.

"Touch it again and I'll hit you over the head with the curtain rod."

Shawn looked over her shoulder and grinned. "I'm fine, just…" She didn't know how to explain it.

Veda tilted her head to the side and stared. "That's not exactly your 'holy shit' face. Your eyes would be bigger and your face all scrunched up."

Shawn shrugged again and her grin widened.

"Wait. You're excited aren't you?" Veda sat back down.

"Something like that."

"Well, I'll be damned. Maybe she's on her way back."

"Huh?" The statement confused her.

"The Shawnna I know."

The Uber had arrived.

Instead of answering, she walked the few steps toward the chair, leaned down, and hugged Veda. "Maybe."

Veda squeezed so hard it was difficult to breathe, but Shawn didn't mind. "Go on. Good luck or whatever I'm supposed to say to encourage a Tinder hookup."

Shawn laughed. Then, a few seconds later, she was out the door.

The upstairs portion of Good Friends was almost empty, so it should have been easy to spot Carmen, but Shawn wasn't having any luck. She was tempted to text her again to see exactly where she was, but decided to try the balcony instead.

Shawn scanned one end and turned the corner to do the same with the other side. She stumbled forward, nearly falling ass over teakettle. The folding chair in her way went sprawling but thankfully, Shawn was able to stop herself from doing the same thing.

"My God, are you okay?"

Well, shit.

She knew that voice. Looking upward, Shawn caught Carmen's gaze.

Carmen's expression was a combination of amusement and concern. Her mouth was slightly open and there was a twinkle in her eyes. "I have to say, though, I'm sure that being on your knees is a good look for you."

Well. Shit, yeah.

"I'm okay." Shawn smiled. "Did you put that chair there so you could laugh at me?"

Carmen shook her head and chuckled. "No. You did a bang up job of making me laugh earlier. This was bonus."

"Glad I could oblige." Shawn slid onto the empty stool across the table from Carmen.

Wrapping her lips around her straw, Carmen took a long pull.

"You started without me."

"I was early," Carmen said.

"I'm gonna take that as a good thing."

"Take it however you want." Carmen leaned back and looked at Shawn with enough intensity to burn.

Shawn took a moment to savor the resulting shiver that swept over her. She held Carmen's gaze until Carmen licked her lips and a saucy little smile formed. "You'd better catch up."

Sliding off the stool, Shawn was intent on doing just that.

"But I did say drink. Not drinks."

Sweet God. This was really going to happen. Shawn turned slightly and cleared her throat. "You did. Didn't you?"

Carmen nodded, and that saucy smile became down right naughty.

Getting a drink didn't seem so important anymore. Shawn took a step forward, closer to Carmen. She didn't know what possessed her to do so, but it felt like the right move.

Carmen's expression was welcoming and sultry.

Shawn slid a hand around Carmen's neck into all that glorious dark hair. She brushed her lips against Carmen's and pulled back slightly. Leaning forward, Carmen sought out more.

"Fuck the drink. Let's go," Shawn whispered before kissing her again. This time, it was hot, messy, and demanding.

Standing at the foot of the bed, Shawn arched forward as Carmen tightened the straps on the harness. Her arousal careened upward several notches. There was something about a woman who knew what she wanted and wasn't afraid to act on it. So when Carmen pulled a black harness and matching toy from the bedside drawer, Shawn was all in.

The overhead light was on, bathing the entire room in its brightness. It was a good thing, because Shawn wanted to see *everything*.

Carmen sat on the edge of the bed and looked up at Shawn with eyes so dark they seemed to swallow her. Her kiss-swollen lips were open slightly and her breathing was shallow, ragged. With steady hands, Carmen placed the base of the toy into the ring.

When Shawn looked down at herself, she started breathing hard too. It had been a long time since she'd done this, so seeing the length of black silicone jutting from between her legs was like something out of a dream.

Carmen pressed her open mouth against Shawn's stomach. Her tongue flicked and her teeth scraped.

As she descended, Shawn brushed the hair away from Carmen's face. She wanted to be able to see.

After sliding her hands around Shawn's hips, she grabbed at Shawn's ass cheeks and leaned forward. Carmen's gaze never wavered. Shawn was riveted.

As the head of the toy disappeared into her mouth, Shawn groaned. The image was enough to heat her from the inside out. Involuntarily, her hips jerked forward.

It didn't seem to faze Carmen as the remaining length of the toy vanished into her mouth and then sprang free, wet and shining. Carmen took her in deep again and again.

Shawn's clit pounded in empathy. "God," she whispered.

Carmen whimpered in return. Her head bobbed back and forth and Shawn's hips started to sway accordingly. After a few seconds, Carmen stilled as Shawn propelled herself forward with more purpose.

Carmen took her, all of her.

The sudden stimulation on her clit caught Shawn off guard. "Fuck!" Somehow, without her noticing, Carmen's fingers had wiggled inside the harness. Her fingertips pressed and swirled, and she wasn't shy about it.

Shawn's gyrating hips increased in speed and intensity.

Carmen never faltered. Her mouth remained firmly wrapped around the toy. With fire in her eyes, she continued to hold Shawn's gaze.

So enraptured by the sensations, the visuals, and the woman, Shawn wasn't prepared for orgasm to hit.

She cried out. Her vision flashed white, and she almost pitched forward but saved herself at the last second.

Carmen moaned.

With a plop, she extricated herself and slowly scooted back toward the headboard, giving Shawn a *come fuck me* look the whole time.

Shawn could barely breathe, but she followed. Now that her head was clearer, she had every intention of savoring this.

Carmen's legs were splayed. She was clean shaven, pink, swollen, and very wet.

Jesus. Shawn's heart was already beating double-time. That sight made it even worse. Not that she was complaining. When she got to the middle of the bed, Shawn sat up and curled her legs behind her. She wrapped her hands around the back of Carmen's knees and yanked her forward, pulling her close enough to touch, taste, and smell.

Using the back of her hand, slowly, gently, Shawn brushed Carmen's sex. She arched forward and whimpered.

Shawn did it again and again until her hand was drenched. It was torture. It had to be.

Carmen clamped her thighs around Shawn's hand, trapping it against her. Unashamed, she undulated against it. "Don't. Tease. Me." Her voice was deep and breathless.

Her movements became uneven, broken. Carmen threw her head back, and as her body began to quake, she let out a series of desperate sounds that went straight between Shawn's legs.

Shawn didn't let her finish. In seconds, she had Carmen's legs over her shoulders.

Carmen gasped then screamed as Shawn buried the toy inside her all the way to the hilt.

"Oh, fuck yes!" Carmen sank her nails into Shawn's back, urging her on.

Shawn groaned. She had to see. She pressed Carmen's legs toward her own torso and peered down. She was mesmerized by what she saw. Shawn slowed her movements and watched as she filled her and retracted only to fill her again.

Good God.

She quickened her pace, and Carmen started muttering incoherently. When Carmen reached down and wrapped her hand around the toy, Shawn nearly lost her mind.

Carmen groaned as the toy slid between them. Then, she pulled it out completely.

Shawn opened her mouth to protest.

"Want you...everywhere." Carmen pushed the toy down further, between her cheeks.

No, this was the part where Shawn was going to lose her mind, but it was in the best way possible. Before this was over, her head was going to explode along with everything else. The arousal she thought had reached its peak twenty times over hiked toward the stratosphere.

Carmen pointed toward the nightstand. Shawn backed away and reached out to open the drawer. Inside was a tube of Astroglide gel. She worked quickly, squirting an ample amount between Carmen's legs. Shawn spread it further, circling Carmen's anus and tantalizing her with the press of her fingers.

Carmen moaned thickly, sending shivers down Shawn's back.

Shawn slathered the toy as well. When she looked back up, Carmen was touching herself. Her fingers slid over her engorged clit slowly, deliberately.

Shawn felt like the sun. She was that fucking hot, but she was going to do this right.

Using well-lubricated fingers, Shawn teased her once more before going inside. She watched Carmen's face carefully as she penetrated her with a single fingertip. Stopping at the first knuckle, she retreated, despite the amount of give. The next time, she got to the second knuckle, moving forward at a snail's pace. Carmen whimpered and gyrated against her, pushing her in even more.

"I can take it. Fuck me," she pleaded huskily.

"Are you—"

"If you have to ask, you're not listening."

Shawn heard her loud and clear, but she had no intentions of just diving in.

After pulling Carmen's legs back over her shoulders, Shawn eased closer and lined up the toy with her opening. With her hand still present for guidance, Shawn gently rolled her hips forward.

"Yesss!" Carmen rubbed her clit harder.

Shawn pulled back slightly and when she pushed forward again, she went deeper. She repeated her movements several more times before she sank into her as far as she dared.

The sounds Carmen made were dirty and uninhibited.

Shawn was drunk with it all. Her head buzzed as pleasure sloshed through her. She glided into her first prolonged thrust. There was no resistance. For the moment, the physical stimulation against her clit was minimal, but the mental stimulation made her feel like everything between her legs was awash in flame.

Carmen moaned constantly. She continued to circle her clit, but her fingers were becoming a blur.

Shawn's hips surged slowly, deeply.

Abruptly, Carmen stopped. Shawn watched in amazement as two of Carmen's own fingers trailed downward and disappeared inside herself.

"Fuck. FUCK!" Carmen cried out.

The sounds of wet slapping flesh was the best music, a symphony of the basest kind.

"Break me."

As if she had been waiting for permission all along, Shawn let go, losing herself. Sweat burned her eyes something fierce, but that pain was inconsequential to the pleasure bombarding her. As her pace increased, so did Carmen's.

Carmen started to tremble. Her hips jerked and bucked. She came with an impressive list of expletives leaving her lips.

Shawn's vision grayed and then lightened spectacularly. Orgasm reached for her, and she could tell already that it was going to beat the shit out of her.

She embraced every second of it.

Sitting on the side of Carmen's bed, Shawn finished draining a bottle of water. She smiled as Carmen trailed a hand down her naked back. Shawn glanced over her shoulder. "I brought you one too. You want it?"

"Mmm, thank you." Carmen sat up against the headboard and accepted the bottled water. "I didn't mean to fall asleep on you like that."

"It's okay. I dozed for a minute too."

"Good to know."

Shawn went quiet as Carmen drank. She was feeling a lot at the moment, but mostly there was a sense of free falling. She knew the earth was beneath her, and that she was going to touch it eventually, but right now Shawn was almost weightless. To add to it, there was a newness. Not concerning the situation. It was something inside her.

"You okay?" Carmen asked.

Shawn leaned back against a pile of pillows. "Yeah, I'm fine. I better get going in a little while, though." It was for the best. She wanted to keep the boundaries clear this time.

Carmen yawned and stretched, drawing Shawn's gaze to the breasts she had barely touched. "Too bad. Keep my number."

Licking her lips, Shawn murmured, "I didn't say I was leaving right this second."

Carmen chuckled.

It was well after eleven o'clock when Shawn sat down in the back of an Uber. Sleep tugged at her, but she resisted. It had been a very eventful night. She looked out the window. Coming from Uptown, the city was alive with lights. She was pretty sure that parts of it never slept anyway. The sight was hypnotizing.

Her phone rang, yanking her from a light doze. Shawn pulled it out of her pocket and answered. She yawned and said hello simultaneously.

"Were you sleeping? I'm sorry for calling so late."

Shawn's heart fell into her stomach, sending acid up the back of her throat. She had expected Veda or maybe even Keisha on the other end. They were the only people she really talked to, but the joke was on her for not checking the caller ID first.

She jerked the phone away and peered down at it. Courtney's name was in lights. All she had to do was end the call.

"Shawn? You there?"

But the sound of Courtney's voice paralyzed her and brought with it a wave of emotion strong enough to keep her that way.

"You're there. I can hear you breathing, and is that a radio in the background?"

"What…" Shawn croaked. She cleared her throat. "What do you want?" Courtney's timing was craptastic. Did she have some kind of sixth sense that let her know when Shawn gained some peace of mind?

"I miss you, and it's confusing as hell. I have to be honest. I think you deserve that. Sometimes I don't know where I stand with Amy, but you were always a sure thing. You never hid yourself from me. Even when we were struggling, I knew what you were feeling."

When the pain struck Shawn square in the chest, it went from warm to icy. The city she was just admiring dimmed. Her senses were blunted toward the outside world, but the mounting ache helped along by Courtney was acute. "You still kept on hurting me anyway."

"I thought being with Amy would be exciting, and it was at first, not knowing what the next day would bring." Courtney continued to talk as if she hadn't heard a thing. "Now, it's hard to keep up. You were boring, safe, and easy to read." Courtney paused. "I'm not trying to be mean or anything."

Shawn closed her eyes. The darkness drowned her. "No," she whispered.

"What?"

"Just no." Fury blasted through Shawn full force. She shook with it. While it was aimed at Courtney, part of it stayed with Shawn. How the fuck did she fall in love with somebody like Courtney? What the hell was wrong with her? Most of all, why was she letting herself get hurt? "Fuck. You."

"You don't mean that. I know you. I know you still care about me, and I know you still want me. Remember how good it was? There was nothing predictable about that. I know—"

"You don't know me. If you did, you'd know our ship sank. There's no getting back on it." She spat the words out like they were rancid. "If you *knew* me, you wouldn't be calling at all." On that note, Shawn hung up. It was a liberating feeling, but it couldn't touch the anger now seeping through her.

CHAPTER 8

AFTER FLIPPING THE SWITCH FOR the garbage disposal, Shawn stared down into the drain. She couldn't see a damn thing, but she couldn't look away. She wasn't one to think of life in metaphors, similes, or whatever, but this one was hard to miss. The disposal growled loudly as its teeth pulverized the food that had been in the sink. She knew what it was to be ripped to shreds. She also knew what it was like to be teeth-gnashing infuriated. It was an emotion she couldn't seem to shake, but it was easier to be mad as hell. Made it hard to feel anything else, which was perfect. The anger wasn't painful, but all the other shitty emotions were. She didn't want a damn thing to do with them.

"SHAWN!"

She jumped at the sound of her name. Shawn quieted the disposal and turned around.

"That place in your head that you were just visiting must have been nice. I swear I've been calling your name for over a minute."

Shawn shrugged. "So. What?"

"Okay, what the fuck gives? You've been all standoffish the past few days. I've been trying to give you space, but that's over. I can't. You have too much going on for me to let it go." Veda walked farther into the kitchen and leaned against the counter. "I think I've heard you speak like twenty words in three days. At least I know your Tinder hookup thingy went well, but…"

Shawn almost shrugged again but was able to stop herself. "I've got a lot on my mind, and I'm trying to get it all straight."

Veda stared. Her eyes narrowed. "What aren't you telling me?"

Sighing, Shawn glanced away. Her gaze landed on the blinking red numbers on the microwave. All the while, Veda studied her like bacteria under one of those expensive-ass microscopes. She fidgeted. The whole thing was a little uncomfortable.

"Oh my fucking shit. Courtney called you, didn't she?" Veda shook her head and balled her hands into fists.

Shawn cringed. Damn her eyes.

"And I bet you talked to her!"

Underneath the surface, something hot flared to life in Shawn. "I don't need you to berate me like I'm a fucking child. I didn't ask for your opinion."

Veda's eyes widened. She reared back as if Shawn slapped her. "That wasn't what I was doing. I was showing concern."

"No, it sounds like you're judging me. I'm fine. I hung up on her. At least that should make you proud." Shawn's tone was snide.

"Whoa!" Veda held up her hands in surrender. "You're not fine. That's pretty obvious. I don't get it. Why didn't you tell me?"

That was a good question. Her reasons were selfish and kind of messed up too. Shawn wanted to hang on to the anger long enough for her to have no more fucks to give. "When I'm ready to talk about it, I will. If not, who says you have to know everything?"

"Okay, okay. Damn. You're right, I guess. Now, calm down." Veda stepped closer. "I am proud of you though." She wrapped Shawn in a hug. "Just don't let her suck you away from the progress you were making."

Shawn stiffened. It took her a few seconds to return the hug.

Stumpy's was actually busy before noon. That was a bit of a shocker, but it kept Shawn occupied. There were at least ten people browsing the floor, and a few minutes earlier, there had been a line for tokens. She couldn't begrudge anybody at this point. Sex felt good in more ways than one. She had been trying to have it as much as possible.

Shawn eyed two women who kept looking her way. She put her elbows on the counter by the cash register and waited for them to get the courage to ask whatever question they were whispering about. After a couple more minutes, they came forward.

One woman, a blonde, smiled. The other woman, another blonde, stared. Her face was all scrunched up as if she'd been sucking on lemons.

Shawn tried to smile back, but she was sure it came out as a grimace. "Can I help you?"

The woman's smile faltered a bit but she stepped forward and whispered, "Yes, um, are the silver bullets on display here all you have?"

Her friend continued to look at Shawn in what she could only assume was disgust. She actually took a step back and clutched her purse.

Shawn snorted. She couldn't help herself. She was the only black person here at the moment, but apparently, that was all this lady needed. Shawn looked heavenward at the new Debbie gracing the swing and did her best to hold on to her composure.

"Um, excuse me?" The smiley blonde tried to get Shawn's attention.

When she was able to look at them again, Lemon-head was whispering something in her friend's ear. Whatever calm Shawn had gained left in a hurry. "You do know I'm in here and you're out there, right?"

"What does that have to do with silver bullets?" Smiley asked.

"I'm talking to your friend who's looking at me and holding on to her purse for dear life. We don't *all* steal, you know."

"What? No. The Internet said this was a bad area. We—"

"Don't even," Shawn interrupted.

Lemon-head grabbed her friend's arm. She really looked scared now. They scurried out the door like their asses were on fire.

Okay, maybe she read too much into the situation, but still. "Fucking tourist," Shawn muttered to herself. She wasn't up for any kind of shit today.

After the crowd died down, Shawn made a choice. Instead of searching for a job, she picked something to watch from her Netflix queue—*The Texas Chainsaw Massacre*. It was off the chain crazy and gory. In other words, it was a mental health movie with a chainsaw and just what she needed. Besides, if there were any new jobs listed, they would still be there tomorrow.

Shawn wasn't even thirty minutes in before her mind started to wander. She'd done her best to deal with the whole Courtney thing on her own by refusing to think about it. The emotional residue left behind was enough. Shawn had expected to be right back where she started, but she wasn't. Did she feel diminished? Small? In a way, but it was nothing compared to a couple months ago. That was obviously some kind of progress. She reached for the brown paper bag behind her laptop. After taking her sandwich out of the plastic wrapper, Shawn poked at it. She wasn't feeling it, but she took a bite anyway. She wasn't boring in any area of her life. Veda didn't think so and neither did Carmen or Keisha.

Unfortunately, Courtney called again the next night. It was pretty late, but when sneaking around was involved, Shawn assumed that was par for the course. She didn't answer. She was hip to the game now. The caller ID had to be checked at all times. Courtney didn't leave a message.

Leatherface revved the chainsaw, and Shawn took another bite of her sandwich. She also picked up her phone. Feeling strangely detached, she pressed her thumb against Courtney's name in the missed call log, and all her contact information popped up. Shawn's finger hovered over the word, delete. Several seconds passed, and she had done nothing.

A woman screamed bloody murder. Leatherface had claimed another victim, while she sat here being all pathetic. Shawn's heart pounded. Maybe she wasn't as detached as she thought. Maybe she wasn't as pissed off as she thought. She was able to hang up. She should be able to do this. Shawn's phone beeped as a text message flashed.

It was from Keisha. Tonight.

She stared at the text. The last time Courtney had called, Shawn made sure she was three fingers deep in Keisha within a couple of hours. This time, she tried to do it on her own, which was a good thing, but there was a shitload of anger bubbling. Fucking Keisha was a damn good way to harness it for a little while.

Yeah. Shawn responded.

Good.

Shawn went back to the screen that held Courtney's information. She glared at it until the words and numbers started blurring together. Her hand trembled, which was a sure sign of weakness that left her pissed off at every little speck of shit human being on earth.

She pressed delete and tossed her phone on the table. For a second, she was triumphant. Then, she got pissed off again. "Goddammit."

Shawn opened her legs wider, straining her thigh muscles. She tangled a hand in Keisha's hair and pressed her closer. Her hips increased in cadence until she was practically humping Keisha's face. Shawn wanted her tongue everywhere, and when Keisha dipped it inside her, she gasped, "Fuck."

Keisha moaned, sending a riot of sensations between Shawn's legs that pushed her even higher than she had been before. Before she had a chance to properly enjoy it, Keisha was sucking on her clit. That shit was frustrating and exhilarating at the same time. Keisha did her best to hold Shawn's hips down, using her nails to dig into her flesh to add to the torture. Shawn was teetering on the verge of orgasm. She gritted her teeth and denied herself.

She wasn't ready.

Instead, she pulled at Keisha's hair. When she didn't stop, Shawn yanked harder. She paused and glared at Shawn from between her legs. The lower half of her face was glistening and slick.

"What?" Keisha asked breathlessly.

"Come up here."

She rolled her eyes but started crawling up Shawn's body. Keisha's hardened nipples left a burning trail over Shawn's stomach. They were both sweaty and sticky. And since Keisha was taking her own damn time, their skin clung in some places and slid in others, but she didn't stop until she was lying completely on top and they were face to face.

When Shawn's hand could reach, she slapped Keisha on the ass, hard, for her impertinence. In return, she whimpered and smiled. So, Shawn did it again and again with pretty much the same results. With a final smack, she trailed her hand down between Keisha's cheeks and went lower still, passing her anus. As she pulled Keisha into a kiss, Shawn plunged inside her.

Keisha's answering groan was long, desperate. She tucked her legs against Shawn's sides and began grinding her hips helplessly.

This moment was something Shawn could get behind. She was all power and control, driving into her relentlessly.

Keisha's hips jerked erratically and with a loud cry, she came all over Shawn's hand.

Shawn jolted awake. It took her a minute to realize that she wasn't at home. She turned over on her back and glanced to the other side of the bed. Keisha was facing away from her. She was obviously sleeping. Shawn sat up.

She had to go.

There was no reason to stay. She had no intention of muddying the waters between them even more than they already were. Yeah, they could totally be friends, and who was she kidding, they could totally be more too. Both were a little too much to handle right now. It was time to re-establish some boundaries.

Slowly, she rose off the bed and as quietly as possible she felt around in the dark for her clothes. They had to be near the foot of the bed where she left them. It didn't take her long to get dressed, but she was missing a shoe.

"Shit," Shawn whispered. Maybe it was in the living room.

"What are you doing?" Keisha's words were slurred with sleep.

Shawn nearly jumped out of her skin.

The covers rustled and Keisha turned on the bedside lamp.

Irritation crept over her, but Shawn was able to swallow it down. "Do you know where my shoe is?"

"No." Keisha drew the word out. "Is something wrong? You're being weird."

"I just wanna find my goddamned shoe so I can leave!" Something clicked, and Shawn went from annoyed to enraged.

Keisha huffed loudly. Her eyes were wide and full of confusion and anger. "What the fuck was that? Where is all this coming from?"

"I don't have to tell you anything. We just—"

"Fuck. I know that. We talk too."

"Not tonight." Shawn was firm.

"And I never asked you to stay the night." Keisha's tone was getting a little icy.

"I know that." She never told her no, either.

Keisha got out of bed. She picked her robe up off the floor, put it on, but left it untied. She leaned slightly to look under her side of the bed. Then, she bent over completely and came back up with Shawn's shoe in her hand.

Shawn reached for it and met Keisha's gaze. Her expression gave nothing away. Keisha snatched the shoe back and held it to her naked chest. "I don't know what's going on, but it's obvious that we need to take a break. I'm not going to let you talk to me that way." Keisha thrust the shoe in Shawn's direction and walked toward the bathroom.

She put on her shoe. Shawn felt empty, numb, but she left anyway. As she walked out of the house, she set up a ride with Uber and decided to wait for it on the porch. Shouldn't she feel guilty for the way she acted? Shouldn't she feel something?

Yeah, probably, but there was only a clinical detachment.

Shawn looked down at her phone. Only a couple minutes had passed, and she had eight more to go. Instead of checking her email or social media, she opened the Tinder app. After swiping left a few times, she stopped and swiped right. Karen looked interesting, and Shawn was going to make damn sure she wasn't bored with her, either.

CHAPTER 9

Now that her early-morning guest, who had been one of four over as many days, had left, Shawn was freshly showered and eager to get on with her plans to do absolutely nothing except sit in front of the TV. She was off work, and she had no intention of losing brain cells by watching daytime television. Maybe it was time to start *Jessica Jones*. Shawn took a sip of her coffee and set the mug on the table.

Shawn needed something to draw her in, because she sure as hell didn't want to think. Shit, she didn't want to feel either. Above her, the floorboards creaked, and she looked up to see Veda coming down the stairs. She stopped midway, looked at Shawn, and then scanned the rest of the area.

"She gone?" Veda raised a brow and waited.

For a few seconds, Shawn didn't say anything. "Yeah."

"Okay. Was that somebody new? She was loud. I thought you were killing her."

Veda smirked at her, and Shawn wanted to grin back, but it just wouldn't come. "Elsie."

"What? That's her name? How unfortunate. It's like naming your child Blanket."

Shawn snorted.

Veda smiled and looked at her with a soft expression in her eyes. "That was good to hear."

"What?" Shawn knew what she was going to say. She wasn't sure why she asked.

"You, laughing. It feels like it's been awhile. You've been so…"

Shawn looked away and reached for her coffee.

"I'm not judging. Promise." Veda held up her hands in the universal sign of placation. She then sat down beside her. "So, it seems like you've really got the hang of the Tinder thing."

After Karen, she hadn't seen any point in holding back. Shawn shrugged and continued to drink her coffee.

The silence between them was tense. Veda barely moved, and Shawn tried to prepare herself for what came next.

"Okay, did I really piss you off that bad? I mean, it's bound to happen. We live together, and I dig for details, especially when someone I care about is hurting. You know that."

"You usually know when to stop, though." Shawn turned her head slightly to meet Veda's gaze.

"I stopped, didn't I? But it's hard. You're not yourself. In a way, you seem worse than you were before, but at least then you were talking to me."

Shawn took a deep breath and let it out slowly. Her shoulders sagged by the time she was done. Was she worse? She wasn't sure. She barely recognized the woman she'd been a couple months ago. Hell, she didn't know this one either. "I don't wanna talk, V."

"Yeah, no shit. Part of me wants to kick your ass until you let it all out."

Shawn huffed in amusement. "I know. It must be killing you."

"It is." Veda drew the word out until it sounded almost snake like. "I hate what she's done to you."

Well, Shawn hated that she let it happen. Nobody else was going to get that chance anytime soon.

"The whole taking care of you thing? I meant what I said."

Instantly, Shawn was aggravated. "I don't need—"

"Yeah, obviously. I'm off today too. What are we doing?"

Shawn had to force herself to relax. This was Veda. "As soon as I get my laptop, *Jessica Jones*."

Veda groaned. "You brought porn home? I love you and everything, but I don't know if it's enough to do that with you."

Another snort escaped. Shawn glared at her best friend.

Veda stood and smiled down at her. "Getting coffee. You want a refill?"

Shawn held up her cup.

Pink

Yawning loudly, Shawn stopped counting the money in the cash register until the fuzziness passed. Phyllis didn't usually bother Shawn on her day off, so she'd been surprised to get a phone call last night, asking her to come in a couple hours early.

It was a little after 6:00 a.m. Who the hell watched porn before breakfast?

Shawn blinked and finished the money count. Afterward, she started on the tokens. When she was done, she yanked off her gloves and set them aside. At this point, she wasn't sure getting up at ass-crack-thirty to catch the bus was worth it. She could have taken Uber, but there was no way she was paying twenty-three bucks. It wasn't worth it, not today.

She sat down and opened her laptop. Then, she went straight to Netflix. She and Veda had watched all but two episodes of *Jessica Jones*, and she was tempted to finish it. At the last second, Shawn decided that doing that would be kind of mean. Veda was annoying the shit out of her right now, but being shitty to her wasn't going to help anything. She queued up something from the BBC collection instead.

Halfway through the second episode, Shawn was enthralled by *Doctor Foster*. That woman wasn't crazy. If the signs of cheating were there, then cheating was happening. She knew that firsthand now. Shawn was surprised she was able to watch this, given the subject matter, but fuck it. She did anyway.

By the end of the third episode, Shawn was blazing mad. The doctor's friends knew? What the actual hell? Her brain went into overdrive. Had any of Courtney's—well, *their*—friends known what was going on? They probably had and talked about it behind her back. After knowing Courtney forever, they were more loyal to her anyway. Fucking bitches. Every single one of them. There was a reason she felt so alone during the last year with Courtney.

People in general were shitty. Shawn was sure of it now. She obviously couldn't beat them. Might as well join them. For the cheating alone, Shawn branded Courtney a horrible person. The fact that she was now calling and texting every week even after their last conversation, even after everything that happened, made her a goddamned soul-sucking vampire. Blocking her number made sense, especially since Shawn continued to ignore her.

Instead, Shawn used each attempt to communicate as fuel of sorts to stoke her anger and her actions.

Shawn's phone beeped. She looked down to see a Tinder notification. She went to her text messages instead, but she didn't have any new ones. It had been a week and a half since she'd heard from Keisha. Shawn wasn't sure how she felt about that. If she ignored all the sex, Keisha was the first new friend she'd made in New Orleans. That was probably all fucked up now. Shawn tried to ignore the growing ache in her chest. She could apologize and try to explain.

It was tempting, but maybe what happened with her was for the best. Shawn opened Tinder. Maybe doing things this way was for the best too.

"You purdy."

He wasn't. Not at all. The man smiled. He was grizzled, wrinkled, and had two teeth missing from the front.

Shawn pulled on gloves. "Token, sir?"

"Not yet. You gone give me the penny tor? Never been hur."

"Sure. If you'll step back from the window…"

The man nodded. He looked so eager. It was kind of disgusting.

"On the far wall to the left," Shawn said as she pointed, "we have all our DVDs. It's an extensive list. The cases are empty, but if you decide to buy one, I can hook you up. The DVDs that play in the back are handpicked by the manager."

The old man scowled, but Shawn kept on going.

"The next couple aisles are all our dildos, butt plugs, vibrators, harnesses, cock rings, cuffs, both fur lined and metallic, riding crops, and so on." Shawn leaned forward and pointed near the back. "That wall houses all our blow-up dolls. Debbie is the most popular."

The man glared at her. "Jus' give me a goddamn token."

Shawn almost smiled. She didn't make a bad Vanna White at all. "That'll be five bucks, and you can stay as long as you want."

The old man grinned again. "Well, all right."

"It's just like the subway. Put your token in the slot on the turnstile, and you're ready to go."

He turned to go, but a few seconds later he stopped. "You can come wit me. I might need someone ta hold my hand." His smile was evil, but his eyes were sincere.

Still, Shawn was sure that his hand wasn't what he wanted her to hold. "Aren't you somebody's grandfather?"

"Well, yeah, but what's that got to do with anythin'?"

Shawn stared.

He waited. "You not comin'?"

"No, definitely not."

The old man waved his hand in exasperation and disappeared in back.

Shawn shook her head. This job was as dead end as it could get, but it was entertaining and distracting. There were also times when it was teetering on fascinating. People of all shapes, sizes, colors, and backgrounds came into Stumpy's. Some were ashamed. Some were amused and horny. Some were obviously lonely, and some probably didn't give a damn what anybody thought about them. People were living their lives right in front of her, and unfortunately, Shawn wasn't doing the same. She sat back, watching, and she wasn't sure that she had the energy or the motivation to do something about it.

The door creaked, and Shawn glanced up at the security feed. She squinted, but it was still a person she hadn't expected to see, especially since she'd seen her a couple days ago. Shawn met Carmen at the window. She studied her and waited because maybe this just got weird.

Carmen smiled. It was slow and sexy. "So *this* is Stumpy's."

"Yeah, what you see is what you get." Shawn crossed her arms and continued to stare.

"Is that right?" Her voice dropped an octave, taking her tone straight out of the bedroom.

Shawn's stomach clenched. The things that woman said when Shawn was inside her and how she said them? Wasn't something she was going to forget any time soon.

"Yeah, that's right. So, what are you doing here?" What kind of woman comes to a sex shop in a pantsuit? She had to admit, Carmen looked good.

Her dark hair was wild and curling over her shoulders. It made Shawn wonder if she let it down especially for her.

"I wanted to check to see if you're free for the next few hours."

"You could've called, texted." Shawn stayed aloof. She didn't smile. Keeping her body rigid, she gave nothing away.

"But then I wouldn't have been able to browse the selection. There might be something I want to try."

Jesus. "Second shift should be here in about a half hour. Maybe I can help you pick something out."

Carmen put her elbows on the counter and leaned forward. "Hope so, but are you gonna let me in? You look bored."

"Yeah, but don't do this again." For the time being, there were some doors that needed to say closed. Shawn flicked the locks. Carmen was there waiting. After allowing her to take a few steps inside, Shawn pressed Carmen against the closed door.

Shawn opened her bedroom door wide and waited for Carmen to step out into the hallway first.

"I'm gonna be late. I have a meeting in thirty minutes." Carmen ran a hand through her hair. "I look presentable, yes?"

"You look fine." Shawn put a hand at her back and steered her toward the living room.

"Good, and don't forget to tell your friend that I didn't mean to drop her hairdryer in the toilet. I was distracted."

She most certainly was. Good thing it wasn't plugged in. They weren't able to agree on an item at Stumpy's, but Carmen had some interesting things in her car. "I told you not to worry about it. I'll get her a new one." Shawn reached out for the front door, but stepped back as it was opened from the opposite side.

"Hey!" Veda's gaze went from Shawn to Carmen. She smiled slightly. "And hey, Shawn's friend."

Carmen breezed past them both. "Nice to meet you. Shawn will reimburse you for the hairdryer." Then she was gone.

Veda stepped into the townhouse and closed the door behind her. "Well, all right then. What did Ms. Fancypants mean about my hairdryer?"

Shawn waved away her concern. "I'll walk to Family Dollar in a few and get you a new one."

"I have another one in my bedroom. It's fine." Veda tilted her head and stared at Shawn. Her forehead was crinkled. "And her name was?"

Irritation jumped to the surface in record time. At the moment, Shawn didn't mind so much and aimed it at Veda. "Does it matter? Really? Shit."

Veda huffed. "Yeah, chew me another asshole because I was trying to make conversation. I can't believe I fucking dared."

Something coiled in Shawn's chest. Maybe she needed a good fight. The urge to lash out was hard as hell to contain. "Whatever." She had no idea how she reined it in, but she did. "It's your night to cook."

"I know that." Veda walked toward the stairs. "You planning on letting that bug out of your ass tonight so we can watch the rest of *Jessica Jones*?"

Even though it had been very little, Shawn had given enough of herself today. "No. Let me know when dinner's done. I'll eat in my room."

Shawn went into her bedroom and closed the door. She didn't wait for Veda's snarky response or her unwanted concern.

CHAPTER 10

Veda leaned against the open door of Shawn's bedroom.

Shawn worked hard, pretending to keep her attention on *Inside*, the movie she'd loaded on her laptop, while warily watching Veda as inconspicuously as possible.

"I know you see me." Veda crossed her arms over her chest.

"Mmm." Shawn still didn't look up. Tonight, she wanted to be left alone.

"I'm gonna talk, whether you look at me or not."

She decided on not.

A few seconds later, Shawn glanced up. Veda was stomping toward her, and before she had a chance to protest, she'd already reached out and slammed her laptop closed.

"Fuck it. I changed my mind."

Shawn leaned her head back against the wall and glared up at Veda. She so wasn't up for this. "What, V?"

"It's that tone like I pissed on your pancakes or something. Things are off between us, and I think we need to reconnect or whatever before one of us says something really shitty."

Shawn sighed and closed her eyes. When she opened them again, she said, "I'm tired."

"I can relate. Hell, I'm on my feet for almost eight hours."

Veda misunderstood. Shawn didn't mean physically tired. She meant mentally. "Yeah."

"Okay then. Let's go get food and we can get drinks after. No, let's do drinks first. I think it would do us both some good. It's been a while since we've been out. You've been busy." Veda rolled her eyes. "I've been—"

Shawn chuckled dryly, interrupting her as it all slid into place. "So that's what this is? You're jealous because I'm spending time with other people?"

Veda sucked in a breath. "Did you..." She shook her head. "Did you just say that out loud?"

Her muscles burned. Shawn's body was rigid with tension. It was almost like she was coiled and getting ready to strike. "Yeah, I did."

"That was an arrogant prick thing to say."

Shawn shrugged.

Veda's face reddened, and her eyes flashed. "You know, you were already a different person when you got here, but there was still some of the old you in there. I don't know who the fuck I'm talking to right now. I knew you were hurting. I can't believe you let her do this to you."

Veda's words were too close to her thoughts, to her own feelings, and it was enough to enrage her. Shawn reared up, meeting Veda face to face. "Mind your own damn business!"

"You are my business, asshole! That's why you're here, remember? To be around somebody who actually cares about you! I tried encouraging you, supporting you, but now I just need to kick your ass. The thing with Keisha actually seemed to be getting you over the hump. So did Tinder at first. But, it's like after every woman you fuck, you get meaner. I'm surprised any of them want anything to do with you."

Clenching her fists, Shawn growled. "You don't know what you're fucking talking about."

"Oh yeah? Then where's Keisha? I haven't seen her in weeks, and you sure as hell haven't talked about her."

Shawn stepped closer. "Leave me alone!"

Veda snorted. "You did something to piss her off, didn't you?"

"We were never going to be together." Shawn threw her hands up in exasperation.

"I know that! But didn't you tell me you liked her and at least wanted to be friends?"

"Who the fuck cares?"

"I do! I care that you're becoming a douchey asshole. I care that you're hurting yourself and other people." Veda's eyes were glassy like she was about to cry, but no tears fell.

"Well, stop! Just fucking stop. I don't need some lonely, pathetic dropout telling me how to live my life."

Veda's mouth fell open. She flushed bright red then went decidedly pale. Her lips trembled and her hands fisted at her side. "I don't care how fucked up you are right now. You don't talk to me like that. Don't look at me. Don't speak to me until you get your shit straight." Abruptly, she turned and left, slamming the door behind her.

Shawn stared at the closed door. Her chest was heaving and her eyes burned. Inside, all she felt was hollow.

She tried to watch the rest of her movie as if nothing happened. While she was exhausted before, now it felt like a thousand ants had invaded her muscles. Shawn couldn't sit still. She stood and as she got closer to the door, she heard the low murmur of the TV.

Shawn hesitated before opening the door. She didn't want to be cooped up in this room anymore, and she didn't want to stare down Veda again. She could do it if she had to. *Had* was the operative word here. Shawn twisted the knob and stepped out into the hallway. When she got to the living room, Veda was there on the couch, watching the six o'clock news.

Veda glanced at her. Her lips pursed and her eyes hardened. It was suddenly so cold that Shawn expected to see a white cloud when she exhaled. After turning away, Veda reached for the remote and hiked up the volume loud enough to drown out the sound of any words she was tempted to say.

Moving quickly, Shawn went into the kitchen. Veda's obvious anger further triggered her own. She had some fucking nerve. All she had to do was listen. Shawn had made it clear she wanted to be left alone. She'd said the words in plain English. In fact, she'd been asking her to butt out for a while now and give her some space.

Shawn yanked open the refrigerator and grabbed the ingredients to make a sandwich—ham, turkey, cheese, and mayo. It was going to have to be her dinner for tonight.

She was *fine*. Maybe a little irritable, but she was more in charge of herself than she had been a couple months back. How could Veda not see that? Mindlessly, Shawn pieced together her sandwich. After putting

Pink

everything back, she searched the cabinet for a Little Debbie. She reached into the Oatmeal Cream Pie box, but felt nothing. She snatched it down and opened it wide.

The damn thing was empty, and she didn't want a fucking Nutty Bar.

Shawn held onto the counter as a wave of emotion tumbled through her. She was all at once pissed off, sad, and full of fear.

Veda could demand help with all the bills instead of just electricity and rent.

She could also kick her out at any minute.

Shawn ripped the empty box to shreds, leaving a mess. She got a Coke and hightailed it back to her room.

Seeing the bruises she left around Carmen's waist and on her ass a couple of days ago didn't do much to stop Shawn from gripping her tighter. In fact, it inspired her to go further. She grabbed a handful of Carmen's ass cheeks for leverage, and pumped harder and faster into her from behind.

The bed shook and slapped against the wall.

Carmen growled and yelped in enthusiasm as if she were in her element.

In the meantime, Shawn was damn near flying. With each thrust, she purged herself of all the anger, the sadness, the guilt, and even the fear, but the kicker was that it all came right back.

Less than an hour later, Shawn sat up in bed, flipped on the lamp next to her, and watched Carmen while she slept. Shawn felt heavier than she had before calling her, but maybe that had more to do with Carmen than with her. Maybe it was time to move on. She'd gotten what she needed from her.

Shawn shook her awake.

"Huh, what?" Carmen jolted upright and blinked sleepily.

"You need to go."

Carmen's eyes cleared. "Shit, I didn't mean to fall asleep."

Shawn stayed quiet and watched as Carmen got dressed. A few minutes later, she yawned on her way to the bedroom door. She waved nonchalantly in Shawn's direction. "I'll call you or something."

"No. Don't." Shawn exhaled slowly.

Carmen stopped and stared. "What?"

"I won't call you. You don't call me."

"Hmm, is that right?" Carmen's expression was blank, except for a teasing smirk.

"Yeah."

Carmen walked toward her. When she got close enough, she wrapped her hand around the back of Shawn's neck and leaned forward. Shawn looked up at her and stiffened, expecting a hard, bruising kiss as a parting gift. She nearly gasped in surprise as it turned out to be a gentle brush of lips. Carmen did it again and again until Shawn moaned and reached out for her.

After pushing Shawn's hands away, Carmen stepped back and whispered, "Your loss. Good night."

CHAPTER 11

SHAWN SHOOK A FEW DROPS of Scary Hot Ghost Pepper Sauce onto her chicken sandwich. After reassembling it, she took a bite. There was a flash of flavor and then her mouth started to burn. Instead of reaching for her drink, Shawn leaned back in her chair. She was used to the sting and kept on eating, rotating between her sandwich and chips. Stumpy's had been quiet all morning. Except for selling a few tokens, there was no typical noon rush.

Everything was fucking quiet. Her townhouse, despite the blazing heat outside, had become Antarctica. When they were in the same room, Veda did her best to freeze her out with a look, an exasperated sound, and body language that screamed avoidance. Veda shrank into herself as they walked by each other as if one of them could be cut by the sharpness between them. Shawn refused to let it bother her. Veda would get over herself soon enough.

Her phone hadn't rung the past few days either, which was fine. Shawn was confident that if she called, someone would come running. She was still getting Tinder notifications, but for the moment, no one caught her eye.

Well, she'd wanted to be left alone, and Shawn had gotten her wish.

Shawn took the last bite of her sandwich and opened her Coke. Her mouth was almost numb, mimicking the way she felt internally. She went back and forth between blistering anger and nothing at all.

The weird thing was, Stumpy's was fast becoming the only place she could relax. One minute it provided solace, and the next total hilarity, courtesy of the customers. Of course, there were times she was disgusted too. Hell, if she stayed here long enough, Shawn imagined she could run through the whole emotional gamut.

The door creaked and Shawn jumped up so fast she nearly knocked over the table in front of her. Instead of glancing at the video feed, she went straight to the window.

"Good afternoon. Welcome to Stumpy's."

After picking up a butt plug, the woman turned toward Shawn and smiled. "Well, thank you. Aren't you sweet."

Shawn blinked. All kinds of people came into Stumpy's, but this was unexpected. The woman was blonde, sporting a pink sun visor, and had her hair pulled back in a flouncy ponytail. That wasn't what caught Shawn's eye, though. It was the words printed on her T-shirt in big, black, block letters: "Proud mom of an honor student at Kimmel Elementary." Pink capris, ankle socks, and Crocs completed her ensemble.

The woman went back to her shopping. Her face scrunched up as she held up two butt plugs. Her lips moved as she examined them, but Shawn couldn't hear what she was saying.

Obviously, soccer moms needed love too. Far be it for her to kink-shame. Shawn smirked. She couldn't help it. This was a welcome distraction. Very welcome. "Can I help you with anything?"

The woman glanced at her again. "Yeah, do you guys have shopping carts of some type?"

This place wasn't Target—not by a long shot. Wal-Mart either.

"Uh, no. Sorry, but you can put your stuff up here until you get everything you need." She wasn't the first person to ask about that. Why didn't they have handheld baskets or something? It was definitely worth bringing up to Phyllis. Most people didn't buy more than a couple items, but still.

The woman nodded and did just that, placing two butt plugs and a harness on the counter. She smiled and headed toward the DVDs.

Shawn was a little fascinated. She wasn't sure why. Maybe she merely needed something to do. Before she realized what she was doing, Shawn had unlocked the office and was out on the sales room floor. Grunts, moaning, and cheesy music filtered in from the back, but Shawn tuned it out. She went to the window and moved the woman's potential purchases to the side to give her more room. She got a good look at the butt plugs. They definitely weren't for beginners.

"Do you need lube? We have an okay selection, but it's nothing to scream about," Shawn said.

The blonde scooped up two movies and walked toward Shawn. Her ponytail swished from side to side. "I didn't see—"

"There's a display behind the counter." Shawn pointed at it even though it was in full view. "Gotta keep it out of sticky hands. It's easy to pocket."

"Understandable." The woman studied the display. Her nose crinkled. "That flavored stuff is disgusting."

Shawn hummed.

"We are running low," the woman mumbled and kept looking. "Oh great! You have it. Let me get a bottle of Slippery Stuff."

She liked the high-end stuff. Shawn could respect that. "No problem."

"I couldn't believe it when I found a Groupon for this place. Usually, it's just for online stores, and I don't like doing that. My kids are way too nosey." The blonde rolled her eyes and chuckled. She had a unique voice: high pitched, perky, with a little something underneath. It was very Jennifer Tilly—*The Bride of Chucky* version, not *Bound*.

A Groupon? It shouldn't have been all that shocking.

"So, you just have the one honor student?" The words rolled off Shawn's tongue. What the hell? She didn't make conversation with the customers, or at least not like this.

The woman blushed. "I actually have two. My little girl is in the sixth grade and my son is in the fourth." She paused and tilted her head to the side. "Do you guys do special orders?"

Shawn blinked again. "Um, I'm not sure. I'll have to call the manager."

"Can you do that, please? Most of these places do, but they try to charge a fortune for it. I hope you guys aren't like that. I like it here, and you've been *so* nice." She gave Shawn a slight smile.

"Let me grab the phone." Shawn moved quickly. She was in and out of the office in a few seconds. She dialed Phyllis's number.

"Thank you so much for doing this." The woman reached out and squeezed Shawn's elbow.

"No problem."

Phyllis answered on the third ring. "Everything okay?"

"Yeah, I have a customer who wants to know if we do special orders."

"You sure we don't already have the item? I got some new toys in a few days ago. They're in the cabinet in the office."

"Not sure. Let me ask her what she's looking for, and we can go from there."

Phyllis sighed. "Okay."

"Ma'am, what—"

"Already on it." The woman pulled her phone out of her purse and showed Shawn the picture.

Interesting. It was a plastic ball with handles and a dick on top.

"It's the…" Taking some liberties, Shawn tapped the screen then swiped her fingers to enlarge the ad. "Hot Dreams Vibrating Sex Ball with Dong."

Phyllis was quiet for a few seconds. "Oh, no, we don't have that. Yeah, tell her we can do it, but it'll be a twenty dollar cash handling fee on top of shipping and the item itself. She can pay for the rest with her credit card. It'll probably take five business days."

"Okay, I'll let her know." Shawn hung up.

The woman's smile was slow and dazzling. Her head bobbed, sending her ponytail swinging. "I heard! That sounds reasonable to me. It would be so much easier if I could come pick it up here."

Shawn thought the woman was going to hug her. "Glad I could help."

"I'm getting these too." The woman gave Shawn the DVD cases.

Ass Up 3 and 4. Somebody had an anal fixation. Nothing wrong with that. It was just strange for a woman who looked like her to be so nonchalant about it. Shawn cleared her throat. "These will be easy to find. The movies are in alphabetical order."

"Well, that's convenient."

"It is."

"Is there a particular color you want the sex ball in?"

The woman nodded. "The black one with the brown dong, I think. Not everything has to be pink." She pointed at her sun visor and laughed. "It has a remote."

Shawn glanced at the woman's head. She was all kinds of confused. "Your sun visor?"

She squeezed Shawn's elbow again and laughed loudly. "No! The sex ball!"

"Oh." Shawn chuckled with her and started moving toward the office.

"When it comes in, I'll have to practice with it. I want to be able to put on a show."

Pink

Talk about letting her freak flag fly. Shawn paused and turned. This woman had a lot to say. Maybe it was like the bartender thing and porn store clerks are easy to talk to about all sorts of exciting porny things.

"Good thing it's deflatable. That'll make it easy to hide from the kids. Once they were old enough to walk and get into things, we had to get a trunk. My husband wanted a padlock. I was able to convince him that a combination lock was a better way to go. Those things are so random and hard for someone who doesn't know the combination to figure out."

"I'm with you on that." Shawn pointed toward the office. "Let me ring all this up for you."

"Okay, thanks. You've been so great."

What did Shawn learn today? Never, ever judge a book by its cover.

When she was alone again, Shawn stepped outside to get some real sunlight. She could have lifted the curtain on the display window but that wasn't the same. She leaned against the open doorway. The heat and humidity were stifling, and for a few seconds, it took her breath away. A streetcar whizzed by, and the sidewalks teemed with people. Some of the passersby, especially the ones with kids, gave her a pointed look after peering in the window. The only thing Shawn could do was shrug.

She people-watched until sweat dribbled down her face. Shawn took one last sweeping look and tried to figure out who was happy, screwed up, or in pain, just by their expressions. She wondered what people could tell about her. Then she decided that she didn't care.

After sitting back down, Shawn picked up her phone to check the time. She was a little taken aback to see a text from Keisha waiting for her.

I'm in Dallas for the next few days at a hair expo. This may not be for the best but let's talk when I get back?

Shawn waited, expecting other emotions to come. Guilt, irritation, something, but she was on empty. She responded to the text anyway. Ok.

She stared at her phone, but Keisha didn't ask how she was doing. She didn't ask how the job hunt was going. She didn't ask anything.

She hadn't heard from Veda either. That was no surprise.

Everything was fucking quiet again.

CHAPTER 12

THEY STOOD AT OPPOSITE ENDS of the kitchen, staring each other down. Shawn was trying to get out and Veda in. Even though they lived in the same townhouse, Shawn had been doing a spectacular job of avoiding Veda. It was simple, really, especially since Veda had been doing most of the work. She hadn't been home a lot. She had other friends. Friends who made her laugh and vice versa. Friends she took care of.

Friend was a goddamn four-letter word for people who said they understood you—people who said they were going to be there, not people who stared down the people they cared about like a red Kool-Aid stain on a brand new white T-shirt.

Shawn clutched at the Coke in her hand. The can was sweating and slippery but it served as an anchor of sorts, giving her a reason to be in this space. Every inch of this townhouse was Veda's. Shawn was a guest, and she was starting to feel like one.

Veda glanced at the drink in Shawn's hand. "That better not be the last one."

Shawn didn't say anything. Instead, she opened the can of Coke, took a long swig, and then shrugged.

It was petty. It was juvenile, and a big-time example of negative attention seeking. None of that kept Shawn from taking another swallow. If she was going to act like one of the petulant teenagers she used to work with, she was going all the way.

Veda rolled her eyes and moved toward the refrigerator. Caught off guard, Shawn went right, intent on getting out. At the last second, Veda changed course too. They didn't crash into each other. The kitchen was too wide for that, but their arms and shoulders brushed as they both went their separate ways.

Shawn felt Veda's gaze. It was heavy and blunt as it smashed into her. Veda frowned. Lines of worry appeared around her mouth and her eyes flashed with hurt, then anger, before cycling back to pain again.

A few weeks ago, Shawn would have caved and ended this standoff. Hell, it wouldn't have even existed. But instead of dealing with it, she pushed her feelings way down to a place where there was only numbness.

She took another sip of Coke and turned away. Maybe it was time to find her own place, but that took money, which meant a decent job. Well, shit. Shawn didn't have the drive to devote to something that wasn't working, like trying to find gainful employment.

Shawn pulled her phone out of her pocket and glanced at the time. Keisha expected her soon, and she hoped that whole thing ended up less complicated than this situation, especially since she was a *friend* too.

After giving the Uber driver a five-star rating, Shawn took her time walking toward Keisha's porch. Keisha wanted them to talk, but Shawn wasn't at all sure if that was what she wanted. Lately, talking led to nowhere and just seemed to make things worse. She snorted. Of course, not talking had the same results. So, what was the damn point? Why waste all that energy when they'll probably end up fucking anyway? If Keisha didn't want anything to do with her, she wouldn't have called.

By the time Shawn rang the bell, she'd made her decision. If Keisha didn't go along with it, Shawn could always call somebody else.

Keisha opened the door. For a few seconds, she stared. Then, she smiled, slowly and brilliantly. "Hey."

"Hey, yourself." Shawn nodded and flashed a quick grin.

She stepped aside and ushered Shawn in.

Keisha turned away, walked toward the guest bathroom, and started removing her hoop style earrings. "I'll reimburse you for the Uber if you want. My first day back after a hair show, I tend to work later so I can meet with my staff. Otherwise I would've picked you up from Stumpy's. I just got home myself."

Shawn was right behind her. Before Keisha could take another step, Shawn had her arms around her waist, and within another heartbeat, she pressed her face-first against the wall. It was as close to the bathroom as Keisha was going to get at the moment.

The earring made a slight clang as it hit the hardwood floor. Keisha gasped and pushed away from the wall. "What—"

Boldly, while nuzzling her neck, Shawn moved her hands upward until they were cupping Keisha's breasts. She put her hands on the wall, arching into the touch and pressing her body into Shawn's. Her breathing went ragged.

It was a good sign that Shawn was on the right track. She brushed her thumbs back and forth across Keisha's hardening nipples, and when they were proudly aroused, Shawn plucked and tweaked. To add fuel to the fire she was stoking, Shawn began to slowly grind her hips against Keisha's ass.

"Fuck! We can... We can talk later."

It was really nice when plans like this came together.

Keisha moaned as she flopped back against the bed. "God, that probably wasn't the best of ideas, but damn."

Shawn hummed and sat up.

"You don't agree?"

"It doesn't matter," Shawn answered.

Keisha sighed. Then, for several seconds she was quiet. "Considering what happened last time, we do need to talk."

"I think we just proved that we can get past it." Shawn did her best not to sound annoyed.

"Maybe, but still—"

Shawn's cell phone rang. It was the most precious sound. She didn't have to answer it, but she was going to anyway. Quickly, she grabbed it off the nightstand and checked the caller ID.

It was Karen, which was ironic since the first time they actually touched base was the last time Shawn had left Keisha's house.

"What's up?" Shawn asked.

"Not much, but you busy?" Karen asked.

Pink

"Not at the moment, but I'm surprised you called. You usually text," Shawn answered.

"Maybe I just wanted to hear your voice. You know it turns me on."

Shawn tried hard not to smile. "I do."

"Can I come over?"

Feeling Keisha's gaze burn a hole in her back, Shawn glanced over her shoulder. Keisha was frowning and her eyes were hard.

"Yeah, give me about thirty to forty-five minutes."

"Okay, see you then."

Shawn eased out of bed and started to get dressed, aware that Keisha was tracking her every movement.

"I heard that whole conversation." Keisha's voice was thick and hoarse.

Shawn pulled her dreads out the back of her shirt and met Keisha's gaze. "I know you did."

"That's all you have to say?"

Shrugging, Shawn sat back down to put on her shoes. "Please tell me you're not jealous?"

Keisha scoffed. "When the fuck did you get so goddamn full of yourself? Who do you think you're talking to?"

Shawn stood and looked down at her. Keisha's face was red with anger. Her hands were fisted in the covers. "It's okay if you are. We've probably been doing this longer than we should."

"No shit, really?"

"Look, I'm gonna go." Shawn needed to get out of here. Something was brewing, and she wanted no part of it.

"The fuck you are!" Keisha tore the covers away and scurried out of bed until she was standing buck naked in front of Shawn.

Shawn groaned. "Don't do this."

"We need to get a few things straight. I know what this is…was." Keisha waved a finger between them. "I never asked for more, and I never wanted it. All I said was we could be friends. I can't give you more than that."

"And if I remember correctly, I agreed, but that also means feelings are involved."

"I know that, you ass! I didn't want to hurt you, and if we'd kept going like we were, things would have—"

93

"Yeah, I know that. It's why I started seeing other women. So, what's your point?" Shawn interrupted.

"Who the fuck *are* you? That's my point. I don't care who you fuck. The Shawn I knew was sweet, humble, and decent. Until tonight, you treated me like a person, and I did my best to do the same."

"Whatever." Shawn threw up her hands. "This was obviously a mistake, and all this still sounds like jealousy to me."

"Then your head is a whole lot bigger than it needs to be. So, let me use short sentences. Maybe you'll understand better. We just fucked. You came."

Shawn rolled her eyes.

"You came hard. Then you rolled over and, right in front of me, made a date to fuck the next woman thirty minutes later."

"Yeah, I was there." Shawn crossed her arms over her chest. The light bulb in her head started to spark, especially after hearing everything out loud.

"I'm not a whore. I know what I want, and I go after it. After what you just pulled, you might as well leave the money on the nightstand. I thought better of you, and I assumed you thought better of me." By the last word, Keisha's voice softened to a husky whisper.

Shawn tried to swallow down the sudden lump in her throat. She'd fucked up. The hurt in Keisha's eyes couldn't be misconstrued. She wanted to say something, but a bigger part of her favored flight instead.

"Just…get out."

Keisha gave her an out, and instead of facing the situation head-on, Shawn ran from it.

On the way home, Shawn's phone rang, and even though she'd deleted Courtney's contact information, she knew the number. She ignored the call and the text that came right after begging to *please call*.

A coldness slithered through her.

Karen cried out and slumped against Shawn. Almost immediately, Shawn pushed her away. It was too much, and she was a step away from

Pink

feeling suffocated. Karen threw a thigh over her and brushed her lips against Shawn's neck.

She wiggled away. There was no way in hell she wanted to cuddle.

"What's wrong?" Karen dipped a hand between Shawn's legs.

Quickly, Shawn snatched it away. "We don't do that anyway, so no."

Karen chuckled. "Can't blame me for trying my luck. I can use my mouth, no problem. I love the way you—"

"No. Not that, either."

"What do you want then?" Karen asked.

"For you to go." Shawn stared straight at Karen.

"Fine. You don't have to be so cold about it." Karen sat up in the bed. "Just give me a minute."

Shawn didn't want to be anywhere near her. She scrambled out of bed. She wasn't sure how she felt right now. Despite what had happened at Keisha's, Shawn had to fuck Karen. She didn't want to disappoint her. She didn't want to disappoint herself.

Ten minutes later, Shawn walked Karen toward the living room. The TV was on, and that meant Veda was home too. Shawn rounded the corner. Veda was sitting on the couch. Armed with the remote, she was flipping through the channels.

Their eyes met. Then Veda glanced at Karen, and shook her head before giving the TV her full attention again.

A potent combination of rage and shame seeped into Shawn's chest. She ushered Karen out the door, and when she turned around, Shawn planned to rip into Veda—to scream, and possibly to beg.

Nothing came out.

Veda didn't even bother looking up again. She put the remote down after she settled on *Law and Order: SVU*.

Quietly, Shawn walked past her, back to her room. She sat on the edge of the bed and covered her face with her hands before pushing them through her hair. She couldn't remember ever feeling so lonely, leaving her tempted as hell to return Courtney's call.

CHAPTER 13

Shawn stared down at her phone. The words there seemed bigger, like they were being advertised on a billboard. Her fingers moved automatically, typing up a response to Tina, a new connection made on Tinder. What was she doing? What the hell was she doing? A little voice in her head encouraged her. It told her she could make this one different. Tina could be somebody she could talk to, laugh with. Shawn was lying to herself, but that lie was so much better than the truth all around her. So, with that in mind, Shawn pushed the lie forward.

Let's meet at Burn for drinks and appetizers. We can see what happens from there.

A few seconds later, Tina responded.

That sounds great, but I think I have a late appointment. Give me a sec let me check.

The door moaned as it opened. Shawn glanced up to see who it was, and before she had time to wonder, Phyllis let herself into the office.

Phyllis smiled. The lines around her eyes and mouth deepened. "Hey, my baby. Surprised to see me?"

"Pretty much. Was starting to think you were just some disembodied voice on the phone."

"You're not the first person to say something like that. Stan sees me the most." Phyllis adjusted her glasses and pointed toward the open door. "Get that box for me. I drove up the same time as UPS. I got some new stuff I wanna do a test run on."

Shawn did what she was told. She sat the box on top of the chipped, gray filing cabinet and went to hunt for a pair of scissors. While looking through a nearby cabinet, Shawn heard a series of clicks and a swish. She turned to see Phyllis piercing the box with a switchblade.

Shawn stared.

Phyllis looked up. Tendrils of hair had fallen out from the messy bun on top of her head. They fanned her face, making her look even softer and more feminine. It was still hard to reconcile that she ran Stumpy's. "What? It's New Orleans. I have a Taser too." She went back to unpacking the box. "Since you're my only female cashier, I wanted to get your opinion."

A phone chirped.

"I think that was me." Phyllis reached into her pocket and took her phone out. "No, must have been you. Guess we have the same notification alert."

Shawn grabbed her phone off the table. It was a text from Tina.

Sorry it took so long to get back to you. I had to go clear some things for my supervisor. I think I should be done by 5pm or so. Does 6 sound good?

She read the message three times in quick succession. That little voice reminded her that Tina could be different if Shawn wanted her to be. She wasn't sure what she wanted or needed. There was a hole inside her that begged to be filled, and now, this was the only thing Shawn knew that worked even a little.

6 is good.

Great! I can't wait. Tina texted, adding a smiley face emoji at the end.

Shawn responded with a smiling emoji wearing a cowboy hat.

Phyllis cleared her throat. Shawn glanced up.

"Okay, now these may not look like much, but keep an open mind."

"I'll try." Shawn gave her a tight smile.

A few seconds later, Phyllis revealed a series of glass dildos. They were exquisitely made, and each one looked a bit different in color and consistency. "Interesting."

"They're made out of crystal. Figured I'd class this place up a bit."

Shawn shrugged. "I guess there's a market for everything."

"There is, but I've been thinking. It's time for Stumpy's to get a website. Maybe feature these bad boys as our top new item." Phyllis picked up one of the crystal dildos and tossed it in the air. She caught it and set it back down. "They're special. It's not just any crystal. It's healing crystal. Blessed by…I can't remember her name, and purified in the waters of some spring."

Shawn's head was all over the place. There was no way she'd heard right. "What?"

"Healing crystal."

"As in, to help broken vaginas? Is that a thing?" The words were out of Shawn's mouth before she could stop them. She was tired and human. Shit happens, but she didn't want to offend.

Phyllis tilted her head to the side and stared. Her mouth twitched. A grin formed, and then she laughed. "Or cure herpes. I don't think either one would be a good tag line."

Shawn chuckled as well. "Sorry."

Phyllis waved the words away. "Don't worry about it. If these things could actually do that? I can't even imagine the amount of money that company would make."

"Yeah, maybe. Can we look into getting handheld baskets too?"

"Like at a grocery store?" Phyllis's nose crinkled.

"Yep, it might encourage people to buy more. The lady that special-ordered that sex ball thingy brought it up. I meant to tell you."

"I'll give it some thought. I guess I've been a bit of a traditionalist about a lot of things."

Shawn nodded. Traditionalism in porn. It sounded like some weird, liberal arts college course. Shawn almost smiled. There were times when she really missed school. She was more naïve back then, and things were simpler because of it.

"One more thing, and I'll get out of your hair. If we get any female customers today, show them the new merchandise. See what they think."

"You want me to keep notes?" Shawn chuckled. Phyllis couldn't be serious.

Phyllis's eyebrows rose comically. "Good idea."

"I… I was kidding."

"I know, but it's still a good idea. I'll throw in an extra fifty for your troubles."

"I always did like doing research. You know, some of the men might be interested too," Shawn said. Fifty dollars wasn't anything to sneeze at, especially in her situation.

"Huh, you have a point." Phyllis smirked. "Make it a hundred. I have cash locked up in my car. Be right back."

Shawn was several minutes late getting to Burn, thanks to the bus. She didn't bother going home since it was easier to catch the connecting bus from work. Good thing Tina had been running behind too and had arrived five minutes earlier, according to her text.

All day, she'd been thinking, rehashing, and analyzing everything that had led up to this point. Courtney's phone call. The falling out with Veda, and the clusterfuck that was Keisha. Shawn had come to one conclusion. They all wanted her to be somebody she couldn't. When it all came down to it, just about everyone in her life was pushing her, and the moment she pushed back they all abandoned her. Being on the outside looking in on this whole thing gave Shawn a kind of clarity. The life she'd been living gave her a type of perspective as well.

She entered the restaurant. Past the hostess desk, it wasn't very crowded, but then again, it was a weeknight. The place was a carbon copy of Applebee's or Chili's. She couldn't decide which one. The hostess glanced up at her.

"I'm meeting someone at the bar."

The woman nodded.

Somewhere deeper in the restaurant, a kid started screaming.

Shawn walked around a couple who were preparing to leave. She glanced over her shoulder as they walked by. They were holding hands. A deep pang of loneliness settled in her stomach. Did she want to be alone? Hell no. Veda had been her lifeline when things first started going to shit with Courtney. Keisha seemed to be damn close to understanding her. Maybe she pushed them too far. Maybe she said and did some fucked up things. Maybe they should've known to get out of the way and let Shawn do her thing. The bottom line was, it all pissed her the fuck off.

Shawn's pocket vibrated. She fished it out. It was a text from Tina.

I c u. I got us a table by the bar.

She didn't even bother to respond. Nothing with Tina was going to be different. Shawn had squashed that little voice not too long after Phyllis left. She walked into the bar area. It was more crowded. Shawn scanned the tables, but at first glance, no one looked familiar. A woman stood and waved in her general direction. Shawn looked behind her to make sure she was the person being greeted.

The woman nodded. It was Tina, but she barely resembled her picture. She was older. Her hair was pulled back into a ponytail, and it was peppered with gray. Not that it mattered, as it only enhanced her attractiveness. Her skin was darker than Shawn's, but it looked flawless. Tina was softer, rounder than the picture she put on Tinder, and the lie immediately put Shawn on the defensive.

Tina smiled as Shawn got closer. The lines around her mouth and light brown eyes deepened.

Shawn didn't smile back as she sat down on the stool across from her. "You could've just been honest."

"I'm sorry. If you wanna leave, I understand." Tina looked down at the table as she spoke.

Sighing, Shawn reached for the drink menu, but decided at the last second that she wanted something a lot stronger than a Hurricane. "It's fine."

Tina glanced up, but her gaze skittered away a second later. "Since you're here, I think you should know I've never done this before. A friend of mine talked me into it. It's been a long dry spell. My ex traded up for someone younger and firmer." Tina chuckled, but then her eyes widened. "Sorry for the overshare. It doesn't seem very sexy to bring all that up." She

Pink

reached for her drink and took a huge gulp. When she sat it back down, her hand was shaking. Shawn couldn't decide if she was nervous or ashamed.

Her story was familiar. Something prickled in Shawn's chest. "Don't worry about it. Say whatever you want." She was going to fuck her regardless.

"You, um, do this all the time?"

Shawn shrugged. "I guess."

"Okay, I guess it's probably good that one of us is experienced with this." Tina licked her lips. "I have to apologize again. I didn't think anyone would…want me like I am now. I looked better back then. I'm actually surprised you stayed. I mean, look at you and look at me." She winced and her shoulders hunched forward.

Shawn's stomach quivered. She could do what she wanted to this woman. Excitement crawled its way up her spine. "Okay. So, you work in home health care?" Shawn pushed on, hoping to lure her into a more normal and easier conversation.

Tina tugged on her earlobe and refused to make eye contact. "I did it again, didn't I? I just need to shut up." She pushed her drink away and reached for her purse, pressing it against her chest like it was going to protect her from something. "This isn't gonna work, is it? I don't know how to do this anymore, and this whole Tinder thing. I don't know what I was thinking."

Shawn leaned closer. "It can work. You're thinking too much. Meet me in the bathroom."

Tina's eyes widened, and her mouth fell open.

After spotting the ladies room toward the back, Shawn stood. It was Tina's choice if she followed. There were a few women in the bathroom. She bypassed them and went directly into a stall. Several minutes ticked by before they left, and then it was quiet. Too quiet. Shawn rolled her eyes, realizing Tina was probably a lost cause.

The bathroom door swished loudly as it opened.

"Hello?"

Shawn's heartbeat accelerated. She opened the stall and crooked her finger.

Tina scanned the area and licked her lips. She met Shawn's gaze briefly and took a long shaky breath before moving forward.

When Tina was close enough, Shawn yanked her inside. Tina gasped.

She had her.

They barely fit, even with their bodies crushed together. Shawn reached behind Tina and locked the stall door.

Tina's breath caught and quickened. "What if—"

Shawn stopped her with a kiss. She wasn't gentle. She wasn't hesitant, and when Tina melted against her, Shawn pulled back.

Tina still wouldn't look at her. "Are you sure—"

In one smooth motion, Shawn spun Tina around, pressed her face-first into the stall door, and let her hands roam over her torso. Tina put her arms on the door and pushed her body into Shawn.

The only sound Tina made was a tiny whimper.

It would have to do. There wasn't a lot of room to maneuver, so Shawn flattened Tina against the stall door and kicked her legs apart. Quickly, she lifted her skirt.

The bathroom door opened. Women entered. They were laughing.

Shawn pulled Tina's underwear down to mid-thigh and squeezed her exposed ass cheeks.

One of the women opened the stall door next to them. She sighed as she peed.

The other one turned on the sink. A few seconds later, the air dryer. "I'm going back out. See you in a minute."

"Okay!"

Shawn slid her hand between Tina's legs, cupping her sex and teasing her clit before diving inside.

Tina barely made a sound except for a quivery breath.

The woman flushed the toilet. When she came out, she stopped in front of their stall. Then, she was out the door. She didn't even wash her hands.

Shawn began thrusting into Tina in earnest. She wasn't as wet as she would've liked, but it would do. With her free hand, she reached back around and slid it under Tina's shirt, over her slightly rounded stomach.

Tina recoiled.

Everything stilled.

"I'm sorry. Please...don't stop."

Shawn hesitated. A familiar combination of anger, sadness and guilt started to rear its head.

"Please," Tina pleaded.

Pink

Growling, Shawn pushed it all away and renewed her efforts between Tina's legs.

"Thank you."

Shawn ignored her.

"Is this…okay? Are you enjoying it?" Tina's voice was soft, quivering.

The ache in Shawn's chest came out of nowhere, and within seconds, it was ripping her open. The situation slowly came into focus. Shawn looked at Tina, really looked at her.

She was glancing at Shawn over her shoulder. When their eyes met, she turned away. Shawn's fingers continued to plunge inside her, but Tina was rigid, unmoving.

Tina wasn't enjoying this at all, and then it finally hit Shawn. This woman's self-esteem was somewhere deep in the sewer, and somehow, Shawn had won the honor of helping her find it again.

This had been her a few months back.

If Keisha had treated her this way, she would have been an even bigger mess than she had been during the breakup. If Veda hadn't been there in the beginning, this would have been her, shaking, scared, and completely unsure.

Instead of somebody like that, Tina got her.

Disgust roiled through her stomach.

To make matters even worse, Shawn had nothing, no one, and that was all her own doing. She backed away until she tripped and sprawled on the toilet.

Tina turned around completely. Her forehead crinkled. She looked confused. "Are you—"

"I'm sorry," Shawn whispered, and those words felt so fucking foreign coming from her lips. "I can't do this."

Tina nodded and pulled up her underwear. Her hands were shaking in earnest, and Shawn noticed that she was trembling too.

"You're a beautiful woman, and you deserve more than a quick fuck in a bathroom stall," Shawn said softly. "You deserve better than someone like me."

Tina met her gaze. Her eyes were glassy, but her lips and chin quivered. She nodded then lowered her head. Without another word, she left.

Feeling nauseous, Shawn turned to the toilet, but there were only dry heaves. She sat back down and wiped at her burning eyes. She didn't even realize that she was crying.

Courtney.

Courtney called her boring. Right now, she wanted to be. Anything was better than who she'd become.

CHAPTER 14

SHAWN HAD NO IDEA HOW long she'd been sitting on the side of her bed. It was still dark out, but it felt like days had passed. Her eyes were gritty, as if someone had poured sand in them. She rubbed them with the heel of her hand, but it didn't help. Crying fucking sucked, in more ways than one. She was drained, unfocused, and her heart was so heavy that there had to be bricks in there, weighing it down.

The guilt, now that she'd let it through, was damn near overwhelming. Shame was next up on the docket, and to round things out was a paralyzing fear. Shawn had burned some bridges. Hell, she blew them the fuck up, action movie style, and she had no idea if they could be rebuilt.

All she knew right now was that she didn't want to do this alone. She should have never tried, but woulda, coulda, shoulda. None of that was of help to her now. Shawn stood and slowly made her way through the hallway and then into the living room.

Shawn hesitated at the bottom of the stairs. She had a choice. To hang on to some semblance of pride, she could sit on the epiphany she'd made and watch everything continue to crumble around her, but where the fuck had pride gotten her? Or she could beg, apologize, and admit that she was more broken than either of them had realized.

Pride be damned. Shawn needed someone. No, she needed Veda in her corner. Was that selfish after everything she'd said and done? Probably. She started climbing the steps but stopped in the middle. Couldn't this wait until morning? Maybe she needed to sleep on it first. She'd be more coherent.

Shawn's body didn't listen. A few seconds later, she was outside Veda's bedroom door. There was soft light shining from underneath. Maybe she was up. She could be reading. She could… Before Shawn lost her nerve, she knocked once and walked in.

"I know it's late."

Veda reared up. Most of her hair was covering her face. "Wha…?"

The man beside her nearly fell out of the bed before righting himself. He looked around the room with wide, confused eyes. It was the naked couch sitter.

Shawn started to back away. "Damn, sorry. I didn't—"

"What the hell time is it?" Veda pushed the hair out of her face and glanced at the bedside clock.

Shawn looked at it too. It was 1:37 a.m.

"What's going on? Why would you—"

"You were right," Shawn interrupted and stepped forward. "You're always right. I fucked up, V."

"This couldn't wait till the sun was up?" Naked Guy whined.

Veda turned toward him. "I'm not trying to be mean, but shut up."

"But—" He sputtered and threw his hands in the air.

"And you need to go," Veda said firmly.

"But, Veda," he pleaded and reached out for her.

"If you want to come back, you need to go." Veda swatted his hands away.

He scampered out of bed.

Shawn kept her gaze on Veda.

After tucking the covers under her arms, Veda met her gaze with a hard stare. "You said some really shitty things."

Shawn stood there quietly. Whatever Veda dished out, she had to take it.

"We've had our arguments, but you never treated me bad. You were a fucking step away from being an abusive asshole. Do you know how close I came to kicking your ass to the curb? It hurt just to *think* about it."

Shawn looked down at her feet. Now dressed, Naked Guy breezed past her and out the bedroom door.

"I knew you were in pain even when you smiled and laughed, but I didn't know how much until you closed me out." Veda scooted to the edge of her bed. "I may be a drop out." Her voice thickened. "But I was there

Pink

for you whenever you needed me. I was prepared to do it again when you moved here."

Cringing, Shawn glanced back up.

"I wish I could say that we're okay, but I've never lied to you. I won't start now, and right now, this isn't about me. You need some—"

"You. I need you." Shawn waved her hand in the space between them. "I did this. I know that. It was easier to blame everyone else." She took a step forward. "I am *so* sorry."

"Yeah, well, I'm human. I don't forgive that easily. Say what you have to say, Shawn. I'm here."

Shawn's eyes burned. She didn't want to cry anymore, but the tears came anyway. "I didn't know. I didn't know how bad off I was. Everything felt…clean after months of being so muddled and bogged down. It was like I was on the outside looking in and nothing could touch me. That feeling trumped everything else."

"Even me?" Veda asked softly, tears sliding down her face.

"Even you."

"You know I love you, right?" Veda asked as she wiped her eyes.

Shawn wanted to go to her. She missed those spontaneous hugs more than ever, but she didn't move a muscle. "S-still?"

"Yeah, fuckface, still." Veda tried to smile but couldn't quite make it. "Just give me some time."

"Okay." Shawn nodded and shoved her hands into the pockets of her cargo shorts. "I don't know what to do now. I know that just because the light bulb came on doesn't mean the lamp isn't still fucked up."

"Mm, true." Veda cleared her throat. "But I guess it's a first step. Speaking of which, I feel like I should apologize. I opened the door to all this."

"God, please stop. I'm a grown-ass woman. I did what I wanted. So, don't even go there."

Veda's eyes narrowed. "What *happened* to you tonight?"

Shawn peered up at the ceiling and took a big shaky breath. "I've done some things, V. I was mean, and tonight, I…" She paused. "I didn't know I had any of that in me."

"Well, now you do."

It got quiet quickly, and there was nothing comfortable about it.

"I should probably let you get back to sleep. We both have work in the morning." Shawn didn't know what to do with her hands. She pulled them out of her pockets, but leaving them hanging didn't feel right. The only thing that felt right was apologizing. Now, there was awkwardness. It had never been that way around Veda before.

Veda nodded and looked away. "Yeah, that's probably a good idea."

Without another word, Shawn left and closed the door behind her.

Shawn tried to sleep. She really did, but she was too wired to close her eyes for more than a few minutes. There was also an overwhelming feeling that she would miss something. It was like she'd been in a state of suspended animation and then been yanked the fuck out of it. With that came the realization of what she'd done to Tina. Had she believed what Shawn said?

Remembering the look in Tina's eyes gave Shawn the answers she needed. Last night had been hard on her, but it had probably been hell for Tina. Leaving her to stew in misplaced blame was the wrong thing to do. Shawn had taken a step toward making amends with Veda, and it was time to take another.

For a second, Shawn didn't know whether to text or call. She made the decision quickly. She couldn't go on being impersonal. It was after 2:30 a.m., but if Tina's nights were even half as restless as hers had been after Courtney, she was up. If she wasn't already awake, Shawn would apologize for that too.

She dialed Tina's number and held her breath as it rang again and again. Maybe she needed to hang up.

"Hello?"

Shocked that Tina actually answered, Shawn pressed the phone closer to her ear. "I didn't think… I know it's late, and I'm the last person you wanna talk to. Please don't hang up."

Tina was quiet.

"You there?"

"Yes." Tina's response was barely a whisper.

"Are you okay? I know it's stupid to ask—"

Pink

"What does it matter?" Tina asked. Her voice was thick and hoarse.

"There's nothing wrong with you." Shawn was firm.

"I—"

"You don't know me, but I meant what I said last night. You're beautiful. I'm the ugly one here. I didn't want any of that to rub off on you."

"What? I don't understand."

"I know what you're going through. I got cheated on too."

"Oh," Tina exhaled shakily. "I don't know what you want me to say."

"You don't have to say anything."

"I need to hang up." A second later, she did.

Shawn stared at her phone for several minutes. She hoped she'd unfucked her part in Tina's emotional black hole but didn't know if she actually had helped at all. She closed her eyes, but sleep still refused to come. Deciding to add to her mounting regrets, Shawn sat back up in bed and reached for her laptop. It had been a while since she opened it for anything other than movie watching, but that was the issue. She hadn't been doing much except women. Pausing for a moment, Shawn acknowledged that it was probably a good idea to pay a visit to Planned Parenthood soon to get checked out. Keisha and Carmen were the only women she'd been somewhat safe with.

Okay, so there was no probably about it. She needed to go.

Shawn logged on to her bank's website. It was going to be bad. No doubt about it. She blinked as she peered at her checking account balance.

"Fuck. Fuckitty. Goddammit."

At first, she'd been saving her paychecks to pad what was already in her account until she could get a more lucrative job. All the Ubers, the dinners, the drinks had taken their toll. She barely had enough money to pay her half of the rent. The truth of the matter was she hadn't looked for a job in over two months, and now she was up shit creek without paddles because she'd sabotaged her own damn self.

With everything else that had happened between them, how was she going to tell Veda? Using words, she supposed. By the time she was done apologizing, admitting that she was a fuck up was going to be easy.

At least there was a bright side to all this. Things couldn't get any worse.

Shawn opened several tabs to job searching websites: WorkNOLA, Indeed, Craigslist, and a couple more. Her intention was to apply for every social service job she could find and was qualified for. Shawn didn't have a choice at this point. She couldn't afford to lay down and wallow in the huge tar pit she was stuck in. She wasn't going out like a damn dinosaur. It was tempting, though, to just let herself be submerged, but maybe she'd gotten the shock to her system she needed to stay afloat.

Her eyes were starting to cross and water. She blinked and glanced around her bedroom. Sunlight poured in through the window, but it was the smell of coffee that really got her attention.

Veda was up.

Shawn closed her computer and pushed it off her lap. She stood and stretched. She was still in the same clothes from the night before and suddenly wanted nothing more than to be clean. It could only help.

Twenty minutes later, Shawn walked into the living room. Veda was already there, watching the Today Show and sipping from a mug.

Shawn swallowed.

Veda looked up, but her eyes were unreadable. Still, she scooted another mug across the coffee table toward her.

"Thanks."

Veda nodded and moved over.

Shawn sat down but teetered on the edge of the cushion. Things were quiet and just as awkward as they had been a few hours ago. Shawn hated it.

"Sleep okay?" Veda asked without looking at her.

"Gave up." Shawn picked up her mug and took a drink of coffee. "I think I was up till about 3 o'clock."

The small talk was painful. Normally, Veda would have already heaped on at least three affectionate insults by now.

"Veda..." Shawn sighed. "I'm pretty much broke."

The quiet extended between them.

Veda reached for the remote and turned off the TV. "What do you want me to say about that?"

"I don't know. Be pissed?"

"Been there. Pissytown is tired of me." Veda chuckled and shook her head. "If things were different, I mean *normal*, between us, I'd tell you to advertise on Craigslist for hand jobs. Fifty dollars a pop."

Shawn smiled.

"But right now, all I can tell you is that I made enough and then some to take care of things before you got here, and I'll be fine when you go."

Pink

It was like someone had poured ice water down her back. Veda's words took her breath away. "Are you telling me to leave?"

Veda glared. "Did I say that? Did you hear those words come out of my mouth?"

"Well, no."

"Okay, have you ever known me to mince words?" Veda raised a brow and waited, but she was smiling softly.

"No."

"Well, there you have it. Don't be a dumbass."

Shawn almost smiled. She may have been starring in her own shitshow, but things were starting to smell a little bit better.

CHAPTER 15

SHAWN PEERED AT THE TEXT from Carmen. She read it several times, letting in sink in. Carmen was the last person she expected to hear from, but there it was in black and white, so to speak.

You made me come so hard. I miss it.

Her insides quivered. It was almost as if Carmen were right there beside her. Three days had passed with no phone calls, no texts and no Tinder notifications. Part of Shawn saw it as a nice reprieve—as time to bounce back to some semblance of herself. The other part of her missed the rush to her ego, to her body and every other part of her that came to life.

There's something about having u inside me.

Christ, this woman did not play fair. Maybe just one last time as a proper transition. Shawn stood in the middle of the office at Stumpy's. She wiped her hand over her face and then continued to stare at the words like they were going to jump out and bite her. Her heart raced and her stomach fell to her knees.

I can be there in 15.

"Oh, God." Both Carmen and Keisha had a way of making Shawn feel like she was walking on water. She *did* miss that feeling, but she had to find a way to start doing that for herself.

Pink

You like breaking me. I liked it 2.

A few seconds later, Shawn's phone started to ring. Carmen's name flashed. Without thought, she answered it, and immediately after, the voice in her head screamed at her for being an idiot.

"I'm already on my way."

Well, shit. "No, no you can't. I told you not to call." Shawn's voice was hoarse, weak.

"You weren't very convincing the last time I saw you, and you're not now either."

"I'm at work, Carmen." Shawn started to pace, walking the length of the office from the door to the cash register and back again.

"So? That didn't stop us before."

"We didn't do anything here."

"You had your hand down my pants. I call that something."

Shawn took the phone away from her ear and stared at it, ordering it and the woman on the other side to behave. She cleared her throat and put Carmen on speaker. "I'm not doing this with you."

"Do you remember the first time? The way you pounded into me..."

She remembered. Shawn closed her eyes. Doing things like this were not good for her. Regardless, Shawn's whole body protested. Her pacing increased. "I don't wanna be mean. I've done enough of that." Irritation simmered underneath her skin.

"Maybe I want you to."

"No!" Shawn was loud, shrill.

Carmen went quiet.

"No," Shawn repeated softly. "I know how this is gonna sound, but it has nothing to do with you."

"Oh please, don't even go there." Carmen sighed. She sounded bored.

"I'm sor—"

Carmen hung up.

After throwing her phone on the table, Shawn plopped down into the chair. She was fucking exhausted and it was barely 11 a.m. She exhaled shakily. She'd come damn close to saying yes, but she didn't. It was a victory and Shawn wanted nothing more than to share it with Veda.

She would be proud, but she wouldn't be *proud*. Things were still tense between them. They were talking, but it was nowhere near the same. Shawn reached for her phone. Before her nerve left her, she deleted the Tinder app, along with a handful of phone numbers. She looked through her cell to make sure she got them all and stopped on Keisha's name.

Guilt climbed its heavy ass on her shoulders. Shame jumped on too. Keisha deserved better than what Shawn had given her, but there was a huge possibility that the last time they saw each other was actually the *last* time.

Shawn didn't want to leave it like that. Keisha's temperament was similar to Veda's in a way. They were both fierce, opinionated, and Shawn got the feeling that if they had the chance to become friends, she'd have Keisha in her corner for life. And, given their most recent conversation, that was all Keisha was emotionally available for. If she was, indeed, available to Shawn at all anymore. Shawn typed three letters and hit send.

Hey.

Minutes flew by without a response. After an hour passed, Shawn accepted that Keisha wasn't going to answer, but she wasn't going to give up.

After hitting send on her third resume today, Shawn leaned back in her chair and stretched. She groaned as her shoulders and back popped, but it felt good. It had been a pretty slow day so far, which gave her a little more time to look for a new job. She should have been doing inventory. However, she still had a few hours in her shift to get that done.

The door creaked. Shawn glanced up, but there was no one there. A few seconds later it opened again. A man entered. He had something wrapped in a tarp and thrown over his shoulder. Shawn stood. What in the pearly fuck? Was it a body? And if it was, why the hell would he bring it here? Her mind went into overdrive, leaving her squeamish and stuck on necrophilia. Also, she'd been lucky so far in that none of her customers had been really threatening and no one had tried to rob her. Stan, from second shift, had

Pink

a few run-ins and so had the overnight guy. Maybe all that was about to change.

Shawn picked up her phone as she watched the man walk toward the window. Now that she had a good look at him, he seemed familiar.

He tapped on the window. "Don't take all day getting up here. I only have thirty minutes."

A light bulb went on as she moved toward the window. It was the white-haired man who'd desperately needed Debbie.

He looked around nervously before unwrapping his package.

Yep, it was the white-haired man and his Debbie. Hard to forget, even though she hadn't seen him since. Debbie still had the tape around her thigh, but there was a lot more than before. Shawn pulled on some gloves. "Can I help you?"

"I've only had her a couple months. I know y'all don't do refunds, but maybe you can help figure out how to fix her?"

Shawn's mouth fell open. Could a person get an engineering degree for this kind of thing? She didn't know what the hell to do and was tempted to call Phyllis since she seemed to be a Jackie of all trades. "Umm, I don't know if I can help you."

"Well, I know what the problem is. The mouth isn't sucking as hard as it used to."

Shawn could do nothing but stare. He said all that with a straight face.

"If you come out here, I can show you." His forehead was already lined with wrinkles, but there was a line between his eyebrows that screamed actual concern for his situation.

Since she'd worked at Stumpy's, Shawn had never backed down from a strange situation, and she wasn't going to start now. They usually had a huge pay out concerning entertainment value and the humanity behind it. She unlocked the office door and stepped out, meeting the white-haired man at the window.

Debbie gaped at her with wide empty eyes, made worse by weirdly smiling lips parted by a rather large hole right in the middle.

"So, she doesn't suck as hard?"

"No. I don't know what happened she was fine one day and then…" He sighed. "Maybe you could order a part or something? Once we figure out which one it is?"

115

Shawn started staring at him again.

"You don't believe me?" The crease between his eyebrows deepened. "I can show you. Stick a couple of fingers in there."

She took a step back. "Not even if I had on ten pairs of gloves, mister."

He rolled his eyes. "Fine. Just watch then. It doesn't even make the sounds anymore."

"Sounds?" Shawn asked.

"Sucking sounds." He gave her a pointed look.

"Oh, okay." How stupid of her. It should have been obvious.

He shoved a finger down Debbie's throat. She made a faint clacking noise. The white-haired man pulled his finger back out. "See, no resistance at all. It didn't used to do that."

Maybe Debbie was tired of being used. Shawn bit the inside of her cheek to keep from smiling. She shrugged.

"Did you see?"

"Sir, I—"

"Just put your finger in there. I swear to God, I'm not making this up."

Well, this was serious if he had to swear to God. "No, I believe you, but I'm still not putting any part of me inside any part of her. Maybe something needs to be reset." Shawn looked around the store. She started walking toward the dildo section and waved for him to follow. She picked up a package-free six-inch toy. "Hold her up."

He did as he was told. "What if you break her?" His gaze was pleading.

"I'll sell you a new one at an employee discount. Twenty-five percent off. That's the best I can do."

The white-haired man nodded.

"Sorry, Debbie," Shawn whispered as she eased the toy into her mouth. Debbie made that clanking noise again, and then came those sucking sounds he was talking about. To test her further, Shawn tried to pull the toy out of her mouth, which took a bit of doing.

"Oh my God!" His eyes brightened and he sounded so excited. "I don't know what you did—"

"I guess it just needs something bigger, wider than a finger."

He glared at her.

"I didn't mean anything by that." Shawn tried to sound sincere. It really was an innocent statement.

Pink

The white-haired man's face turned blotchy red. "Well, what am I supposed to do?"

Shawn had to take a second. The humor of the situation was catching up to her. "Uh, we have penis extenders or sleeves." She took a few steps to the right and took one off the rack to show him.

His eyes bulged out of his head. The man looked like he was about to have a stroke.

Shawn bit the inside of her cheek again, hard, but laughter bubbled out anyway. She covered her mouth with her hands and mumbled, "Sorry."

He threw Debbie over his shoulder and marched for the door, forgetting his tarp. Somehow, Debbie got twisted. She stared sightlessly at Shawn like she had a couple of months before.

It was obviously a cry for help.

Shawn laughed even harder, and God did it feel good. She couldn't remember the last time that happened, and the lightness that tagged along was something she had sorely missed.

The white-haired man turned toward her. His faced was scrunched, and it couldn't get any redder. "I'm reporting this to your manager."

She held up a placating hand. "I'm so, so sorry. It's not you, really. There's just a lot going on."

He still glared.

"Look, I know you don't have time today, but how about a free token? You can use it next time you come in." Shawn smiled at him.

He was mad as hell, but after a few seconds his shoulders sagged and he nodded.

The door opened. He moved quickly, trying his best to cover Debbie back up.

Shawn snorted. She wasn't trying to be mean. Really. Giving him a wide berth, she went back to the office. He met her at the window.

"Oh, wait." He turned back and walked quickly toward the sex-toy aisle and snatched a penis extender off the shelf.

Shawn almost started laughing again. "Twenty-five percent discount for your troubles, sir."

The white-haired man smiled.

She smiled back and meant it. Whether he knew it or not, in the last few minutes, he'd helped her tremendously.

CHAPTER 16

VEDA STOOD AT THE STOVE, flipping a pancake. Her back was to Shawn, which made it easier to speak to her but didn't ease the tension in Shawn's shoulders at all. They were stiff enough to make her neck hurt. She moved her head from side to side, hoping that it would help.

"I have a job interview on Monday," Shawn blurted out.

"Oh, yeah?" Veda didn't turn around. "How many pancakes do you want?"

The tension quickly transformed to disappointment, making her shoulders sag instead. "Three, please."

Veda turned and glanced at her, before plating the first pancake. "We're so polite, aren't we?"

"Isn't that better than what we were before?" For some reason, Shawn dreaded the answer.

"You mean the name calling and the petulant playground bullshit? No, I don't think so. That was us being honest about being pissed at each other." Veda poured batter into the skillet and it sizzled. She shifted her body sideways, meeting Shawn's gaze.

"Well, I wasn't mad at you. I don't think. Everything was more focused inward. It still is. I'm just figuring out how to handle it better."

"I *was* angry at you. Still am."

Shawn could totally understand that. "I didn't mean anything I said."

"I know. Doesn't make it hurt any less. You knew which buttons to push." Veda poked at the pancake with the spatula. "Did you figure it out?"

"What? My shit?"

Veda nodded.

Pink

Shawn leaned against the opposite counter by the sink. "No, not really, but I'm trying to face up to it. That's something, I guess."

Veda hummed and sighed. "I'm trying. You know? I just have to get out of my own way. I really know you didn't mean any of it, but I still think of myself that way...a lot."

"You're one of the smartest, most giving people I know, once you get past the hard candy shell." Shawn wanted to reach out to her. She curled her hands into fists instead.

Veda laughed. "Tell that to my mother."

"I will. Next time she calls." Shawn smiled.

"I might take you up on that."

Despite the positivity in their conversation, Shawn still felt somber. She was tired of all the weight on her. She had to get it off somehow. "Keisha's not talking to me at all, and I don't blame her. She's not the type of woman to tolerate what I did."

"First, get the bacon ready to go in the microwave. Then, tell me what you did." Veda paused. "If you want."

Shawn folded several slices of bacon in paper towel and told Veda everything.

Veda sucked in a breath. "Yeah, you fucked up, but it's good that you wanna fix it."

"She was always up front with me. She listened and treated me like I was important, no matter what we were doing. She reminds me of you. I think that's why I don't wanna let the whole thing go."

The microwave beeped, and Veda plated more pancakes.

"You sure?" Veda asked.

"Yeah, I mean, I guess. The fucking around part of our relationship is over. If we'd kept going..." Shawn took a breath. "At least on my end, there could've been more. She's the kind of woman you get addicted to."

"Huh, how do you know being friends with her won't do the same thing?"

"I don't, but it's worth a try. I'll give her some time. Hopefully, she'll come around and at least be willing to talk."

"Hopefully or not." Veda didn't sugarcoat her response.

"Hey, V?"

"Yeah?"

"Courtney's been calling and texting just about every week. There were times when I really wanted to answer her, but I didn't. I didn't block her because I needed that anger. Otherwise it hurt too fucking much." Shawn said the words in a rush. She needed to get them off her chest.

Veda looked at her for what seemed like hours. Smoke plumed behind her and the smell of burned pancakes filled the kitchen.

"Shit!" Veda moved the skillet to the sink. She scooped the pancake out and stuffed it down the garbage disposal. As she ran water in the skillet, she glanced at Shawn. Her expression was open except for the crinkle in her forehead. "Well? What do you feel now?"

"I don't know, but I don't wanna be angry anymore. I don't wanna be hurt, either."

Veda nodded. "Okay. Now tell me about this interview." She changed the subject like she somehow knew Shawn was getting tapped out. Of course she knew.

Veda knew everything.

From the street, Shawn looked up at the building she was about to enter. It looked like all the other highrises downtown: tall, nondescript, and an ass-load of windows. The only difference was that this one belonged to some Catholic charity. More than likely they weren't going to hire her. Shawn didn't wear a dress or a pants suit. She was dressed in nice pants and a matching shirt. No makeup. There was nothing remarkable about the ensemble but it fit her. She wasn't at all feminine, but she wasn't overly masculine either. Overly being the operative word. Shawn was comfortable, and she wasn't about to set a clothing precedent that could come back and bite her on the ass. They either liked her this way or no way at all.

Sweat started to dribble down her face. It was time to go in. Shawn had traded shifts with Stan to do this interview. If it was a bust, at least she could say she tried. That was the most important thing right now: trying. She smiled at the security guard as she signed in, and by the time she got to the elevator, she'd cooled off. She stood behind a small group of people, and when the elevator opened she was the last one in.

"Hold it! Hold the elevator!"

Shawn pressed the button, and a woman entered.

She smiled. "Thanks."

"You're welcome." Shawn looked at her a moment longer than was polite.

The woman didn't seem to mind. She was looking at Shawn too.

"Wonder Haven."

"Huh?" Shawn asked.

"That's where I know you from. That group home in the Garden District. They had those stupid psych tests?"

"Ohhh!" It all slid into place. Those green eyes and glasses. Her hair was long before. Now, it was short and sleek. "You weren't in the final interview."

"Nope." The woman's full lips curled up in a smile, revealing dimples. "Apparently, I've been harboring a lot of anxiety. I'm glad they were the ones to catch it." She rolled her eyes.

Shawn laughed. "It is their job to help people."

The elevator stopped. They moved to the side to let some people off.

"Mmhmm, I'm *so* lucky. Obviously, you didn't get the job." The woman raised an eyebrow.

"Thank God. That place gave me goose bumps. Plus, that sweaty guy kicked my ass in the final interview. He barely gave me a chance to talk."

"Well, I'm sure he'll fit right in. I don't look good in polos and should've left immediately after I saw that."

Shawn's eyes wandered over the woman. She was petite but curvy. The pant suit only helped matters. "Probably. You work here?"

"Not yet."

Shawn groaned. "You're here for an interview. Aren't you?" She definitely looked like someone they would hire for a case management position. Dressy, professional, with the right amount of makeup even though it looked like she wasn't wearing any.

The woman chuckled. "Yep, I take it you are too?"

"Uh-huh." Shawn sighed. "You're not making me feel hopeful. It's been months since Wonder Haven, and you haven't found a job yet."

"Oh, I have one. Another group home hired me about a week or so later. The place is horrible so I'm looking on the sly for something better."

More people got off.

"What's the name of the place? I gotta make sure I don't apply."

"New Hope." The woman adjusted her glasses.

"Thanks. I'm Shawn by the way."

"Myka." She smiled again.

The elevator stopped for the third time. Shawn glanced up at the floor number. "This is our stop."

Myka shook her head. "Nope, I'm two floors up."

Other people left the elevator. Shawn held the door open. "Well, I feel a little better about my chances now. Good luck."

The elevator started to beep. Shawn let go.

"You too!"

Forty-five minutes later, Shawn left the building. If an interview went beyond fifteen minutes, it was a good one, in her opinion. She wondered if Myka was still up there. She texted Veda and started walking toward the bus stop. There was no point in taking an Uber home.

"I can sell you a token, but you'll have to come back later. The cubicles are full."

"Whaaat?" The man frowned, making his forehead wrinkle. "I'll buy one and wait. How long do you think it's gonna be?"

Shawn bit her tongue to keep from asking him if he wanted to make a reservation. Only the best service at Stumpy's. "No idea. It just depends."

"On what?"

Shawn blinked. The answer should have been obvious. "Some men take a minute. Some take longer."

He glared at her for a second. Then, he grunted and slid her a five. "I plan on being in there for a while."

Shawn stared, because really? Her life was so much more enriched with that knowledge. She gave him a token and went to sit down. The past few hours had been busy. She hated second shift. She'd only worked it once before, but the later it got, the more customers she had. People got off work and came to get off in a different way entirely. She'd already done her job search for the day, so she'd fired up a movie when she first came in. Unfortunately, she only got to watch the first twenty minutes of *The Autopsy of Jane Doe*, but it had been enough to pique her interest.

A little over an hour later, she was done. "Well, damn." The movie had been a surprise but a very good one. She wondered if she could talk Veda into watching it. Shawn smiled and acknowledged that the two of them had made some headway. She reached for her phone, but instead of texting Veda like she intended, she texted Keisha.

I'm sorry.

Shawn started another movie while she waited. Thirty minutes later, Keisha still hadn't responded. It was hard to choke down the disappointment, but she had no choice in the matter. She had to swallow it.

CHAPTER 17

"Friday at two o'clock. I'll be there. Any special instructions?" Shawn asked the clinical director as she consciously leaned back in her chair in an effort to sound and be as casual as possible.

"None at all. I look forward to meeting you."

"Me too. Thanks for the opportunity, Mr. White."

He chuckled. "You say that now. I'll see you soon."

Shawn smiled as she ended the call. She liked him already. Not many prospective employers displayed humor, especially the dry kind. He called at the right time. She needed some good news. She hadn't heard a peep from the last organization she interviewed with, which wasn't the best of signs. To top it all off, Karen had texted the night before, and saying that Shawn had been tempted was a gross understatement.

Whatever residual high Shawn had been riding was dwindling, and she really wanted a fix, no matter how miniscule. Her motivation was waning, but she thought about where she'd been and what she'd sunk to. She thought about Tina and what she'd almost done. It all bolstered her a little, and she hoped that was enough.

A customer tapped on the window. Shawn got up. "Can I help you?"

"Yeah, I think I left my glasses in the back yesterday. Did anybody turn them in?"

"I'm not sure. I'll check." Shawn put on gloves. If they were here, there was no way she was going to touch them after they'd been marinating in God knew what. She looked in the cabinet underneath the register as well as the other obvious places.

Her phone beeped, but instead of picking it up, Shawn met the customer at the window again. "I didn't see them, but give me a description of them. I'll leave a note for the other shift."

Pink

Shawn sat back down a few minutes later after adding to the message on the corkboard already waiting for Stan. She grabbed her phone and pressed the home button. The relief that shot through her settled in her chest as something warm and solid.

I hear you.

It was a text from Keisha.

Do you? Shawn responded.

Yes, ur sorry.

I really am. Ty for talking 2 me I probably don't deserve it, Shawn texted.

You don't. I should just let this go.

Ur the first person I met in a while that's been real with me.

What am I getting out of this? Keisha asked.

A friend if you want one. I know everything else is over.

Five minutes passed before Keisha messaged her again.

Idk if ur worth it. Give me some time. Plz don't call or text. I'll contact u if I wanna talk.

Ok.

What else could she say? She had to respect that. The probability of something positive coming out of the whole clusterfuck pushed her higher, but the reality that she might not hear from Keisha again helped Shawn to stay close to the ground. Maybe that was where she needed to be anyway. Trying to fly had gotten her into trouble.

"Hey, it's not your turn to cook, but it smells good." Veda grabbed the spoon on the counter and dipped it into the simmering red sauce.

After adding another pinch of salt to the pot, Shawn stepped to the side to give her room. "I know, but since I'm usually home first I thought we'd celebrate."

Veda blew on the spoon before putting it in her mouth. "Mmm." She smacked her lips. "Did you put hot sauce in there?"

Shawn shrugged. "Enough to give it a kick."

"Uh-huh, long as it doesn't give me heartburn. What are we celebrating?"

"I got a job interview on Friday. Can you put the pasta in the water?"

Veda opened the box of angel hair pasta. "Really? No shit?"

"No shit. I guess things in the social work field are picking up. Could have something to do with school starting back soon. It's weird. I barely noticed that July had come and now it's almost gone."

"You were all caught up. Maybe next year we will get a chance to celebrate the Fourth like we should have a couple weeks ago."

Again, guilt met Shawn head-on and shame came in from the rear. "Caught up, yeah, that's a nice word for it." Keeping her gaze down, she turned from the stove and moved toward the refrigerator to get the garlic bread out of the freezer.

"I didn't say that to make you feel bad."

"I know." Shawn glanced over her shoulder. "It is what it is."

Veda nodded in agreement. Shawn would have given anything for a hug or even a shoulder bump.

They walked around each other but worked in tandem to get dinner situated. It was nice and damn near comfortable.

"Ugh, I'm gonna go get out of this uniform and wash Taco Bell out of my hair."

"Okay, everything should be ready by the time you come back down."

Veda left the kitchen and headed for the stairs.

"Hey, V?"

"Huh?" She stopped and turned around.

"Keisha texted me today."

Pink

"Oh, and?"

"Don't know yet. She said she needs some time." Shawn bunched and squeezed the dish towel in her hands.

"You gonna give it to her?" Veda raised a brow and waited.

"Yeah, I am."

Veda smiled. "Good. Be back in a few minutes."

Shawn's cell phone rang. It was loud enough to jerk her out of a deep sleep and make her heart race. She blinked until she could focus and stared at the nightstand. Except for the moonlight coming in from the window, her phone was the only source of illumination. She reached for it and looked at the caller ID. Shawn wasn't surprised to see Courtney's number.

On impulse and out of sheer irritation, she answered. "What? What the fuck do you want?"

"You answered. I-I can't believe it. Hey, how are you?" Courtney was smiling. Shawn could hear it in her voice.

"Small talk? Really? It's one in the morning. Girlfriend not home?"

"I drove by our old house a few weeks ago." Courtney went on like she hadn't heard a thing. "Remember that cactus we bought for the porch? It was our first plant. Did you take it with you?"

"Nope. Trash." What was the point of this? What did she think going down memory lane would do?

"Oh. Did you keep any mementos?"

Shawn laughed. She honest-to-God laughed. "The pain. I kept that."

Courtney sucked in a breath.

"You can have that back, though. I don't want it anymore." Shawn waited for all the anger and the hurt to barrel into her. It came, rolling into her like a wave, but it didn't drown her. She could breathe. She could fucking breathe.

"Shawn—"

"Don't Shawn me. I need you to listen. We'll never be friends. We'll never be anything. I'm gonna go live my life the best that I can and you're gonna go live yours. You will *not* call or text me anymore."

"But—" Courtney started to sputter.

"I'm hanging up now." And she did. A moment of panic seized Shawn, but she refused to let it over take her.

Courtney called right back, but Shawn pressed ignore. Her hands shook. She took a deep breath and blocked Courtney's number. The anxiety came back with a vengeance but it was mixed with relief and resignation.

She stared down at her phone. The screen went black, making her bedroom a little darker. A couple of pieces of her that had been scattered slid into place, but there was more of her dangling out there. Shawn pressed the home button again and was thankful that she was whole enough to finally realize that there had been light around her all along.

She just had to let it in.

As Shawn walked out of the kitchen, sipping from her own cup, Veda came in.

"Coffee's made."

"I know; I smell it. Check you out, Mary fucking Poppins." Veda smirked. "If she were black and had dreads."

Shawn chuckled and leaned against the counter. "I don't think Disney had me in mind."

"No, look what they did to Ellen, back in the 90s." Veda filled the mug Shawn had left beside the coffee pot.

"But she showed them all in the end, didn't she?" Shawn watched her friend pour in a boatload of sugar.

"Damn right she did." Veda glanced at her. "You look tired as hell."

"Been up for a while."

Veda set her mug down, put her hands on her hips, and stared.

Her stance stirred up a shitload of affection. Shawn smiled and shook her head. Veda was being her normal pushy self without the words. "Courtney called last night."

Veda pursed her lips.

Shawn's tried to swallow down the hard lump that abruptly clogged her throat. "I, uh, said what I needed to say, and then, I blocked her number."

There was no verbal response, but Veda's eyes widened.

It was weird saying all that out loud. Somehow, the situation became more real. For a second, Shawn couldn't breathe. Then, a bolt of warmth shot through her chest.

It only took four steps for Veda to get to her. Shawn counted. Suddenly, she was enveloped in one of those hugs she'd missed so much.

Shawn sobbed.

Veda held on tighter.

CHAPTER 18

SHAWN RATED THE UBER DRIVER and got out of his car. She glanced across the street and ignored the prickly sensation at the back of her neck. Of all the office space probably available in the City Park area, this agency, Phoenix Rising, Inc., chose to be damn near across the street from Old Fellow's Rest cemetery, but maybe that was for a reason. The cemetery was abandoned and hidden behind a crumbling gate and high walls, but still, those kinds of cemeteries were the creepiest ones. Any horror movie buff knew that. All it needed was a vulture sitting on the gnarled tree outside and some tumbleweeds to complete the picture. She stared at it for a moment longer. She was definitely going to talk Veda into doing the Haunted Cemetery Tour someday soon. Shawn smiled and took a deep breath.

It was time to put her game face on. She was determined to blow these people away. The job was hourly contract work with pre-teen and teen boys that were in danger of getting lost in the juvenile system. If the company was as laid back as the guy sounded on the phone, Shawn had this in the bag. She was twenty minutes early, but that wasn't a bad thing. It could score her some points. The building only had four floors, and unsurprisingly, there wasn't a security guard in the lobby.

Instead of the elevator, Shawn opened the door to the stairwell. Hopefully, the exercise would loosen her up even more. As she rounded the corner on the first flight, a door slammed somewhere above her and the click of heels on concrete let her know that someone was on their way down. She got to the second floor and stopped to stare at a familiar face.

Myka laughed. "This could turn into some new form of stalking."

"For real. I was thinking the same thing." Shawn shook her head and smiled. "I can't believe that Catholic place didn't call you back for one of the case manager jobs."

"Why? You don't know my qualifications."

"True, but I'm sure you have the look they want. Fresh-faced and classy. No offense."

"None taken. I might have to put that in my cover letter next time."

"So, what is your background? Seems like something I should know since we're both going after the same jobs."

"And not getting them."

Shawn chuckled. "True."

"I have a bachelor's in sociology and social work. I have a lot of experience with street kids. Didn't help me here, though. I tanked the interview. I've been on so many of these things they all start to blur together, and I lose focus."

"I know what you mean. Sounds like we both might be stuck at our current jobs for a while. Although, I actually like mine most of the time. It's the pay that makes me cringe. I have to say, though, that New Hope looks way better on a resume than Stumpy's."

Myka took a few more steps down until they were pretty much face-to-face. She tilted her head and grinned. "You remember all that? We've only talked the one time."

Shawn shrugged. "I guess you made an impression."

"Hmm." Myka's eyes brightened and dipped slowly from Shawn's face to the rest of her. "I guess I did."

Shawn's face heated, and she hoped to God that it didn't show.

Myka's smile widened.

Obviously, it did.

"So, did you mean Stumpy's Sex Emporium?" Myka asked.

"Uh, yeah. Look at you getting it right on the first try." Suddenly, Shawn didn't know what to do with her hands so she shoved them in the pockets of her pants.

"I've passed by that place more than a few times. Why the hell is it pink?"

"No idea, but I asked that same question once." Shawn laughed.

Another door slammed above them.

Myka looked down at her watch. "What time is your interview?"

"At one o'clock."

They both shifted to the side to make way for a person who was headed down. Shawn brushed against Myka. "Sorry."

"Nothing to apologize for." Myka leaned against the wall. Her green eyes darkened.

"I like your hair, by the way. I barely recognized you before. Uh, not that it was bad or anything." Shawn almost rolled her eyes because what the hell was wrong with her? After all that damn practice, she should have been smoother than this, but maybe deep down, she didn't want to be. She didn't want to be the slick, overconfident, douchey butch who had a prefabricated line for every woman.

Myka pressed her lips together, but she was still smiling. "It's okay. I know what you meant." She took a step forward and looked at her watch again. "It's Denton."

"Huh?"

"Myka Denton." She held out a hand.

Shawn took it. Myka's skin was soft and her handshake was firm. She pulled away slowly, dragging her fingers across Shawn's hand, leaving a tingle behind.

"Green." Shawn cleared her throat. "Shawnna Green."

"You only have a few minutes, but let's exchange numbers. I'm curious to see how…" Myka's grin went up in wattage. "Well, honestly, I'm just curious."

"Um, about?" Shawn asked. She wasn't sure if it was a moment of panic or stupidity. This woman was flirting with her, and here she was flailing in the wind.

Myka laughed, but she didn't turn or move away. "About you."

Was this about sex? She so didn't want this to be about sex. That would be extremely disappointing.

"We should talk. Maybe go out sometime." Myka bit her bottom lip.

Shawn almost sagged in relief. Was she ready for this? She wasn't sure, but it wasn't like Myka was proposing marriage. "Uh, yeah. Yeah, that sounds good."

Myka opened her purse and fished out her phone. She typed in her code and gave it to Shawn.

Pink

The screen was already on contacts. Quickly, Shawn put in her information. Their fingers brushed again as she was handing it back, and the tingle returned.

Myka paused for a second. Their gazes met. Slowly, Myka glanced down at her phone. She tapped a couple of keys.

"Your pants should be vibrating in a second."

Sure enough, they did. Shawn had turned off the ringer on the drive over, but Myka didn't know that. "I feel it."

"Good." Myka walked around her and continued down the staircase. "Break a leg. Can't wait to hear how it went."

Shawn turned to watch her descent. "Thanks."

It was after five o'clock when Shawn got off the bus near their townhouse. She could have come straight home after the interview, which had gone extremely well, but instead decided to walk around Delgado's City Park campus to clear her head. It was a community college, but the place was still huge. Being there made her nostalgic for the simplicity of college life. Things could be simple again. Shawn was sure of that, especially if she had good people in her life.

She was working on it.

However, for now, her head was still spinning a little about the whole Myka thing, but it was what it was. Shawn wasn't going to overanalyze or ruminate. As she neared their section of townhomes, Shawn saw a guy with big white bags at their front door.

"Hey! Can I help you?"

He turned. "You Veda?"

"No, I—"

Veda opened the door, and Shawn ducked around the man and Veda to enter.

Veda smiled. "Look at that. Right on time. I got Take Out Taxi from Copeland's to celebrate."

Shawn sat on the couch as Veda signed the receipt. "I don't even know if I got the job."

After closing the door, Veda set the bags on the coffee table. "I know that, but you're missing the point. This is a general celebration. A shitload has happened the past few weeks. I wasn't sure if you'd wanna go out, so I decided to bring it to you."

"Awww, that's so sw—"

"Shut up and eat your food. I made sure to get you something you could slather with hot sauce," Veda said. She started emptying the bags and shoved a couple of containers in Shawn's direction.

Then it hit her. Veda was taking care of her again. Shawn wasn't sure if she ever really stopped.

"How did the interview go?"

Shawn smiled. "Mr. White said I was a pleasure to talk to, and he was impressed that I didn't give him the same old tired answers he usually gets."

"Oooh, that sounds promising."

"I hope so. He said I could be called for a second interview by next week." Shawn unwrapped a plastic fork. "I've kinda had an interesting day."

Veda opened her container and scooted back on the couch. "Oh yeah? Do tell."

"The whole Myka thing—"

"Wait. What's a Myka?" Veda's forehead scrunched in confusion.

"A woman I met. We seem to keep going after the same job." Shawn smiled. She couldn't help it.

Veda stared. "Tell me everything." She hesitated. "I mean—"

"No, I want to."

Several minutes later, after Shawn had finished her explanation, Veda asked, "You gonna call her?"

Shawn met her gaze. "Yeah. Yeah, I think so."

"From what you've said about her, don't be surprised if you hear from her first."

Either way, Shawn was looking forward to talking to her again.

CHAPTER 19

"I JUST GOT THE BEST NEWS ever."

"Already? It's only a little after 9 a.m. Good morning by the way." Shawn paused the movie she'd started, so that she could give Myka her full attention.

"Good morning to you too. Now, are you sitting down?"

"Yes, it's what I do most of the day at Stumpy's. Glad my ass isn't flat." Myka sighed. "Really?"

Shawn chuckled. "Sorry, go on. Let's hear your good news."

"I got that state job! The one with child protective services. I nearly forgot about them. It's been over a month since I interviewed."

A horn beeped in the background of Myka's call, followed by a slamming car door.

"You're shitting me?" Shawn smiled so hard it nearly hurt her face.

"No, I'm not. God, I almost screamed in that poor woman's ear. I already called New Hope, but I only gave them a week's notice. I really wanted to give them the finger and tell them to shove it so far up their collective asses that they could taste my hand lotion."

"Well that's not very professional." For someone who looked so innocent, Myka could let shit fly. Shawn really enjoyed the hell out of that part of her.

"I can't be *on* all the time, but I can try for this job since I'm going to be making close to sixty thousand a year." Myka was breathless and giddy. Her excitement was contagious.

"Ho-ly shit."

"I know, right." For a second, loud music filtered between them. "Sorry," Myka said. The sound went down dramatically.

"Maybe you can write me a kick-ass reference letter."

"I'd be glad to, especially if you don't get that job at Phoenix Rising."

Shawn rolled her eyes. "Don't remind me. I still haven't heard from the guy."

"Yes, you have. You got a second interview. You just have to wait till he's back in town."

"It's a group thing. I'm not good at those, so I'm gonna need a shitload of luck," Shawn groaned.

"I think you'll be fine."

"Mmm, where are you headed?" Shawn leaned back in her chair.

"Taking a fifteen minute break to do a Starbucks run. Thought I'd celebrate with a six dollar coffee drink."

"High roller."

"That's me." Myka sighed again. "The only negative thing is I have to go to Iowa for three weeks for training."

"What? How can they train you in Iowa to work in Louisiana? It's like another country down here."

"I don't know." Myka sounded petulant. "But it's what I have to do. That's not going to keep us from talking. It doesn't matter where I am."

"Oh, I know."

"I'm actually surprised at myself. I didn't think I'd like this whole telephone thing. I'm not the most patient person in the world, but it's been interesting getting to know you this past week."

"I'm not boring you?" Shawn cringed. Some part of her had to ask.

"Not at all, but I do think we need to step things up a little."

"How so?"

"It seems like I saw you more when we were strangers. We need to at least have drinks this week and when I come back from Idaho—"

"Iowa." Shawn's phone beeped quietly, but it was only a text notification. It could wait.

"Iowa, thanks. We should definitely do dinner. You think you're up for it? Or am I pushing too hard?"

Sometimes, Shawn needed to be pushed. Since moving to New Orleans, she'd gone from self-imposed famine to gluttonous feast. There was no in between. Now, she was trying to find the middle ground. Maybe someone showing her the way was a step she needed to take. "No, let's do it."

Pink

"You sure?" Myka's smile came through the phone.

"I'm sure."

"I was hoping you'd say th…" Myka paused. "Shit, hold on. That's work calling me."

"Okay." Shawn took the phone away from her ear, intending to check her texts while she waited, but before she had a chance Myka spoke.

"I'm back." Her voice was faint but audible.

"That was fast," Shawn said once she had her phone back in place.

"Yeah, I gotta go. Apparently, I can't leave for a few minutes without shit hitting the fan. I have to make some calls. Get back to you later?"

"Okay."

Totally distracted by the conversation that just ended, Shawn sat and stared down at her phone. She was doing this. She was really doing this. Of course, she had no idea what *this* was. Regardless, it was happening. Myka was funny, smart, and she listened. She had already pulled things out of Shawn that it was probably way too early to reveal, like some of the shit she'd done the past couple months and the train wreck that was Courtney. The most interesting thing was despite all that, she kept calling.

Shawn's phone rang, and after looking at the caller ID, she snatched it up, hoping the caller didn't have a change of heart and hang up.

"Hey," Shawn said hesitantly.

"You… You didn't answer your text." Keisha's voice was soft and tentative.

"I was on the phone, but was just about to check it. I didn't know it was you."

"Now you know."

"How are you?" Shawn asked. Small talk seemed like the way to go.

"I'm fine. The more important question is, how are you?"

"I'm better," Shawn said with conviction.

"Mmm, it's probably better if we get to the point."

"Just as blunt as ever." Shawn almost smiled.

"Always." Keisha paused. "Anyway. Regardless of your apologies, I still don't know if anything, even a friendship, is a good idea, but I'm willing to talk. Phone only for now. I still think you're good people, but I've been wrong before."

It was something. "Okay, I can do that."

"Good. So, have you found a new job yet?"

"No, I've been on quite a few interviews though. I slacked off for a while. A lot of things have—"

"I'm not ready for you to be all chatty again. I'm sorry. Just…not yet."

Shawn pressed her lips together and took a deep breath through her nose. "I get it." She cleared her throat. "Maybe I can learn to listen more."

"What do you mean?"

"I'm saying that friendship is a two-way street. If we're gonna do this, you have to talk too."

"Mmm."

"You're good people too. I've been wrong before, but I don't think I am this time. What I know about you, I can fit into my back pocket." Shawn was nowhere near satisfied with that.

"You might not like—"

"So fucking what? Who the hell am I to judge?"

Quiet stretched between them.

"We'll see," Keisha said instead of answering Shawn's question.

"Yeah, we will."

"I need to go. I have a customer coming in the next hour. You take care."

"You too." Shawn said, but Keisha had already hung up.

She sat her phone on the table. Things seemed promising on several fronts. Shawn couldn't ask for better than that.

The door screeched as it opened. Shawn looked up at the video feed to see a group of men entering. They shoved and poked at each other. She rolled her eyes at their antics.

Frat boys, more than likely.

Fun.

Someone knocked on the window.

Shawn sighed and stood.

A young man smiled at her, showing perfect white teeth and sporting a man bun. He looked like he'd rolled out of an Abercrombie and Fitch ad. "Good morning, ma'am."

Did he just ma'am her? Shawn blinked. "Yeah, welcome to Stumpy's. Can I help you?"

"Sex dolls. Do you sell 'em in bulk?"

"Let's get Debbie!" One of his friends yelled from the other side of the store.

"All right! I hear you," he yelled back. "Sorry about that. So, do you sell Debbie in bulk?"

What the hell was it about Debbie? Shawn nodded. "I think we can arrange that."

Shawn knocked on Veda's bedroom door before peeking inside. "You decent?"

"Hell, no. I'm always a little dirty." Veda turned as she put her hair up in a ponytail. "What's up?"

"You have on pajamas." Shawn couldn't help but be disappointed but the little moons on Veda's shorts were cute as ever.

"I have on pajamas." Veda raised a brow. "You're a fucking genius."

"Shut up. Take them off."

Veda's mouth twitched.

"You know what I mean. Let's go out. I have a shitload to tell you, and I don't wanna sit at home while I do it."

"Something juicy?"

It was about Myka and Keisha, so that was a given. Shawn nodded. "Yeah, it's pretty juicy."

"Hmm, and when you say go out, you mean what?"

"A drink or two? I don't really have the money to—"

Veda waved the words away. "Don't worry about that. I'm just glad you wanna go. It's been a while."

"Yeah, it has."

"Give me fifteen minutes before you order an Uber. Where are we going?" Veda started pulling up her shirt.

"Don't know. Let's go to the Quarter. We'll play it by ear."

"Sounds good."

Shawn turned around and left her to get dressed.

Thirty minutes later, Shawn slid onto the back seat beside Veda. As they sped through the neighborhood, Shawn looked out at the scenery even though there wasn't much to see—mostly apartment complexes and fast food chains, including the obligatory Popeye's Chicken. She'd seen all this a hundred times before, but this evening, things looked different. Everything was a little brighter.

She glanced at Veda and caught her staring. Shawn smiled. "I'm okay."

"I know you are. I just worry."

Shawn nodded in acknowledgment. "V?"

"Hmm?"

"I love you. You know that right?"

Veda grinned. "I know. So, Good Friends?"

Shawn had truly come full circle. She'd taken what she thought was the road forward a few months ago at Good Friends after meeting Keisha, but ended up steering herself off the main track and onto a crappy shortcut. Now she was back on a different path, a better one. It made sense to return, even if all she did was look back to see how far she'd come.

"Yeah, Good Friends."

EPILOGUE

"Excuse me." Shawn said several times as she worked her way to the front of the bus. It was crowded as hell. People stood in the aisle, holding on to the railing above their heads. When she got near the bus driver, Shawn crouched a little to follow the street signs to make sure she didn't get off at the wrong stop like she had on her first day of volunteering. Walking several blocks down Chef Mentuer Highway wasn't the safest thing she'd ever done. Shawn had been dripping sweat by the time she got to the correct address. Well, at least she had made an interesting first impression on the kids. She hoped this third time would be a charm.

"Right here, please."

The bus driver nodded and slowed right in front of the community center.

She got off the bus, took a deep breath, and wondered how many kids would show up this time. Hopefully, it would be more than five. The group could be anywhere from one to fifteen. She set her hopes high but also tried to be realistic. Yes, she'd made an impact the first time she met with the group. Shawn had seen it in their eyes, but there could always be mitigating circumstances. These kids were poor and often had more responsibility than a pre-teen should probably handle. In Indiana, she would've gotten paid for this kind of work but not much. Here, in Louisiana, Shawn ran this teen group strictly on a voluntary basis three times a week. It was a way to keep her skills honed and get some fulfillment at the same time. Stumpy's was, well, a sociology experiment waiting to happen, but working with kids was where she needed to be.

She was tired of waiting for a job to come through. After finally completing the second interview at Phoenix Rising, Shawn still hadn't heard anything two weeks later. For some reason in New Orleans, it could take up to month or more to get through the whole employment process, which sucked ass.

From the front pocket of her backpack, her phone chimed. She fished it out to see a text from Myka. Shawn had at least thirty minutes left before the kids started to arrive, so instead of going in, she sat on the stairs.

FFS I'm going to murder my supervisor the next time she talks to me like I'm stupid.

Shawn laughed out loud.

Will help chop up and hide the body. I don't mind a lil blood.

Myka replied with a kissy face emoji.

I knew there was a reason I liked u.

Shawn smiled as she typed.

I'm ride or die in case u didn't know.

Thanx for letting me kno hav fun w the kids. Call u later maybe we'll hav chance 2 do dinner this wknd.

K.

Shawn continued to grin. Felt like it was creeping up to her eyeballs. Slow. They needed to take it slow. Friends first before anything else. It was a bit old fashioned but after everything, necessary. The good part? Myka was willing to take things centimeter by centimeter.

Shawn turned and looked over her shoulder as the glass doors creaked open behind her. Two men walked out. Shawn scooted more to the side to give them room.

Later, her phone rang while she was in the middle of group. All the kids laughed at her ring, a revving chainsaw. That's what she got for trying

Pink

something new. Shawn shrugged and apologized. Over an hour later, she walked the last kid, Rodney, toward the door. He had been a straggler after the previous sessions and Shawn'd come to expect it.

"Texas Chainsaw Massacre as in Leatherface?" he asked. "I remember you said you liked scary movies.

For a minute, Shawn completely blanked. "Oh yeah. You're right. That movie's older than you are. How did—"

"He's on my Mortal Kombat XL game. I looked him up when I found out all the characters." Rodney adjusted his glasses.

"So, you're a gamer?"

Rodney shrank before her eyes. His shoulders sagged and he crossed his arms over his chest. "I know I'm a geek."

Shawn smiled down at him. "Nothing wrong with that. Let your geek flag fly."

He uncrossed his arms and rolled his eyes. A tiny smile eased its way out.

After cleaning up their area, she gathered her things and made her own way out to the bus stop. Despite being late afternoon, the heat was stifling and the humidity made it feel like someone was breathing down her neck. Shawn checked her phone as she walked. The number looked familiar but she decided to listen to the voicemail before returning the call.

"Hey Shawn, it's Maurice White. I'll be in the office till seven so feel free to call me back if you hear this before then. I wanted to formally offer you the position. We can discuss pay and a start date when I hear back from you. Everyone was—"

"Holy shi—" Hanging up before the message finished, Shawn stopped walking and stared down at her phone. She had over an hour to call back but seriously needed to marinate in everything first.

"Ms. Shawn! You gon miss da bus!"

At the sound of her name, Shawn looked up. A couple of her kids along with quite a few adults were filing on to the bus. "Hold up!" She ran the rest of the way.

Shawn waved and smiled at the kids as she made her way toward the back. With no more seats available, she found a patch of railing to hold on to. The thing was, once she started smiling, it was hard as hell to stop. So Shawn didn't even try. Warmth and relief expanded in her chest. She took a deep breath and let it out slowly, enjoying the easiness of it. If this was the only thing to work out, she could deal. Her livelihood, sense of self and accomplishment were just as important as any of her established or potential relationships.

Veda. She took out her phone again. Shawn had to tell her. For months, Veda had done her best to be there. Shawn wanted her to bear witness to what she helped to facilitate through her patience, her forgiveness, and when needed, a kick in the ass.

With portions of her life still so up in the air, it was nice to touch some part of the ground, and right now, that was all she needed.

ABOUT KD WILLIAMSON

KD is a Southerner and a former nomad, taking up residence in the Midwest, east coast, and New Orleans over the years. She is also a Hurricane Katrina survivor. Displaced to the mountains of North Carolina, she found her way back to New Orleans, where she lives with her partner of ten years and the strangest dogs and cats in existence.

KD enjoys all things geek, from video games to super heroes. She is a veteran in the mental health field, working with children and their families for more than ten years. She found that she had a talent for writing as a teenager, and through fits and starts, fostered it over the years.

CONNECT WITH KD WILLIAMSON
Blog: kdwilliamsonfiction.wordpress.com
E-Mail: Williamson_kd@yahoo.com

OTHER BOOKS FROM YLVA PUBLISHING

www.ylva-publishing.com

BLURRED LINES
(Cops and Docs – Book 1)

KD Williamson

ISBN: 978-3-95533-493-2
Length: 283 pages (92,000 words)

Wounded in a police shootout, Detective Kelli McCabe spends weeks in the hospital recovering. Her only entertainment is verbal sparring matches with Dr. Nora Whitmore, the talented and reclusive surgeon. Two very different women living in two different worlds. When the lines between them begin to blur, will they run from the possibilities or embrace the changes they bring to each other's lives?

CAST ME GENTLY

Caren J. Werlinger

ISBN: 978-3-95533-391-1
Length: 353 pages (100,000 words)

Teresa and Ellie couldn't be more different. Teresa still lives at home with her Italian family, while Ellie has been on her own for years. When they meet and fall in love, their worlds clash. Ellie would love to be part of Teresa's family, but they both know that will never happen. Sooner or later, Teresa will have to choose between the two halves of her heart—Ellie or her family.

GETTING BACK

Cindy Rizzo

ISBN: 978-3-95533-395-9
Length: 239 pages (73,000 words)

At her 30th college reunion, Elizabeth must face Ruth, her first love who bowed to family pressure long ago. As they try to reconcile with their past, Elizabeth must decide whether she is more distrustful of Ruth or of herself. Is she headed for another fall or does she want to be the one who walks away this time? It's not easy to know the difference between getting back together and getting back.

STONE GARDENS

Lois Cloarec Hart

ISBN: 978-3-95533-541-0
Length: 334 pages (110,000 words)

For years, Grae has been trapped in a purgatory of her own making. She spiralled from privilege to the dregs of society. But eventually the world she's held at bay beckons. Just when her life appears solidly back on track, misfortune strikes again. Will Grae run in the face of adversity? Or will the love of family, friends, and one special woman prove that her fate is not written in stone?

COMING FROM YLVA PUBLISHING

www.ylva-publishing.com

THE ART OF US

KL Hughes

Eighteen-year-old Charlee Parker met the love of her life in a parking lot—a leggy brunette with a valedictorian medal hanging from her rear-view mirror and an attitude as biting as a Boston winter.

Alexandra Woodson was guarded, a nineteen-year-old orphan set on a bright future in hospitality administration. She never imagined an art student with a penchant for cheesy pick-up lines and stealing parking spaces would crack her rigid exterior and claim her heart.

For four years, theirs was an enviable love—evergreen and growing. Unbreakable…

Until it broke.

Alex's job now brings her back to Boston, after five years working on the opposite side of the country. When, by chance, they meet again, Charlee and Alex are swept up in a whirlwind of heart-rending history, tossed between past and present, and lovers old and new. Will their lingering connection be enough to convince them that some loves are meant to last? Or should the past remain in the past?

Pink
© 2017 by KD Williamson

ISBN: 978-3-95533-878-7

Also available as e-book.

Published by Ylva Publishing, legal entity of Ylva Verlag, e.Kfr.

Ylva Verlag, e.Kfr.
Owner: Astrid Ohletz
Am Kirschgarten 2
65830 Kriftel
Germany

www.ylva-publishing.com

First edition: 2017

No part of this book may be reproduced, scanned, or distributed in any printed or electronic form without permission. Please do not participate in or encourage piracy of copyrighted materials in violation of the author's rights. Thank you for respecting the hard work of this author.

This is a work of fiction. Names, characters, places, and incidents either are a product of the author's imagination or are used fictitiously, and any resemblance to locales, events, business establishments, or actual persons—living or dead—is entirely coincidental.

Credits
Edited by Jove Belle, Zee Ahmad, and RJ Samuels
Proofread by Paulette Callen
Cover Design and Print Layout by Streetlight Graphics